The Hardy Boys
in
The Crisscross Shad

This Armada book belongs to:

_____

_____

_____

The Hardy Boys Mystery Stories

The Crisscross Shadow

Franklin W. Dixon

Armada

First published in the U.K. in 1972 by William Collins
Sons & Co. Ltd., London and Glasgow.
First published in Armada in 1976 by
William Collins Sons & Co. Ltd.,
14 St. James's Place, London SW1A 1PF

This impression 1977

Printed in Great Britain by
Love & Malcomson Ltd., Brighton Road,
Redhill, Surrey.

There was a loud, splintering noise and the door gave way

CONTENTS

·1·

A Strange Sale

"I WANT to speak to my nephews Frank and Joe Hardy at once," said an excited voice on the telephone. "It's urgent."

"Yes, Miss Hardy," replied the manager of Bayport High's football team. "They're out on the field. I'll get 'em."

Meanwhile, on the thirty-yard line Coach Devlin was saying, "Okay, team. Let's run through our defensive play once more."

The eleven lined up—the regulars on defence, the scrubs facing them.

"86X," barked Frank Hardy, captain and quarterback, as the opposing centre moved over the pigskin.

The ball was snapped. At the same instant, stocky Chet Morton, the regulars' stalwart centre, pulled out of the line to cover the left flank. The scrubs' halfback darted up and over the line of scrimmage.

"Tackle him, Chet, tackle him!" shouted Frank.

Chet ploughed into the second-string ball carrier and brought him to the ground for no gain.

"Good going, boys," said Coach Devlin. "I think you've got that defensive play down pretty well. Once round the field and then into the showers," he said, dismissing them.

Frank and his brother Joe, a year younger, jogged along together. Lithe, blond-haired Joe, who played left half back, was puffing.

"Coach really had us working on that 86X, didn't he?"

"I'll say he did," tall, dark-haired Frank replied. "But it's going to come in mighty handy when we play Hopkinsville—"

"Frank! Joe!" the manager called out. "Telephone call for you. Better hurry. Your aunt seems very excited!"

The brothers looked at each other wonderingly. Sons of Fenton Hardy, the famous detective, they were accomplished sleuths in spite of their youth. They had often received urgent calls but never in a locker room!

Joe hurried to the phone. "Hello," he said anxiously.

"Joe, is that you?" asked a crisp feminine voice. "This is Aunt Gertrude."

"What's up?"

Aunt Gertrude, who was staying at the Hardy home, was the boys' favourite relative. Though she did not hesitate on occasion to reprimand her nephews, they had great respect for her insight into human nature.

"There's a strange salesman in the house," Aunt Gertrude reported. "He's trying to sell your mother some leather goods, but I don't like his looks. I'm sure he's a swindler. I've seen his picture somewhere in the papers."

Joe whistled softly. "We'll come right home, Auntie," he promised.

The boys did not wait to shower or change their clothes, but hurried to their convertible.

Since their father was in San Francisco on a secret mission—so secret that he had not even told the boys its nature—Frank and Joe felt a protective responsibility towards the two women at home.

As he manoeuvred the sleek car through Bayport's busy streets, Frank looked puzzled.

"I don't like this at all, Joe," he said.

"Let's take a look through the window before we go in," Joe suggested. "You know what Dad says. A little undercover sleuthing in advance is better than barging in head-on."

"Good idea."

When they reached the tree-lined neighbourhood where the Hardy home was located, Frank proceeded cautiously.

"We'll park here," he said, quietly turning off the motor and gliding to the kerb about three hundred feet from the house.

The boys went up a neighbour's driveway, crossed the back garden, and approached their own house from the rear.

"How about looking in the side living-room window?" Frank whispered. Joe nodded.

The boys flattened themselves against the side of the house below the window. Cautiously they lifted their heads until their eyes were on a level with the sill. A strange man, his back to them, was there alone.

Suddenly Joe gave a start and said, "He's just taken something off Mother's desk!'

"What is it?" Frank asked. "I can't make it out—oh, yes—it's Dad's key case!"

As the youthful detectives watched, the man, unaware that he was being observed, opened the case and quickly slipped a key off one of the rings.

The boys did not wait to see any more. They dashed round the corner of the house, unlocked the front door, and ran into the hall.

"Why, hello, boys," a pleasant feminine voice said. Mrs Hardy was descending the stairway. "What brings you home so early from practice—and in your football uniforms?"

"Hello, Mother!" they answered together as they followed her into the living-room.

Joe burst out, "This man is what brings us here."

"I don't understand," she replied as the stranger stared at them with an air of surprise.

"Why did you pick up my father's key case and take a key from it?" Frank asked sharply.

"What do you mean?" the stranger demanded angrily.

"Frank! Joe!" their mother exclaimed, taken aback by her sons' actions. "You'd better apologize to Mr Breck. I bought a new key case from him for your father."

"And I was merely transferring the old ones to the new case while your mother went upstairs for her purse," Mr Breck said triumphantly.

Embarrassed, the boys looked at the two cases. There were three keys on the new one.

"Here is a letter of introduction that Mr Breck brought from Mrs Wilson," their mother quickly explained as she handed them a folded sheet of paper.

Her sons scanned the typewritten letter, which told what a reliable man Mr Breck was and how reasonably he was selling fine handmade leather articles. At the bottom of the page was a signature which the boys recognized as that of an old friend of their mother and father.

As they looked up, Mr Breck gazed straight at the boys. A taunting smile outlined the lips of the dark, burly man who was about thirty-five years old.

"No reason to get excited," he said smoothly. "I've just been showing your mother some beautiful hand-tooled leather—"

Breck stopped speaking and looked flustered when he saw Miss Hardy in the doorway. Tall, stern Aunt Gertrude stood there glaring in unfriendly fashion. But the salesman recovered himself quickly.

"Oh, another customer," he said.

"Indeed not," stated the boys' aunt firmly. "Laura," she addressed her sister-in-law, "are you sure this man is—?"

"Oh, please," Mrs Hardy begged, greatly distressed.

Meanwhile, Joe had been silently counting the keys. He did this twice to make certain how many were there. He knew the exact number there should be because Mr Hardy, shortly before he left, had given the keys to his wife in Joe's presence. The boy's sleuthing instinct had prompted him to count them at that time. Now one key was missing!

"Mr Breck," he demanded, his eyes flashing, "what did you do with a thin brass key that was in this old case?"

"Why . . . why . . ." the stranger stammered, hunting for words. "How dare you accuse me of stealing!"

"There's a key missing—a special one. Hand it over!" Joe insisted.

"I haven't got it, you young whippersnapper," the man replied indignantly.

"Please!" Mrs Hardy interrupted. "Mr Hardy no doubt removed the key himself."

"I'm not going to stay here and be insulted any longer!" Breck exclaimed in anger.

He moved to his small suitcase, tossed his samples inside, and snapped it shut.

"I'm getting out of this house," he said hotly. "I've had enough of your insinuations."

Joe made a move to detain the salesman. But his mother forbade it.

"Let him go, Joe," she advised. "No key is worth such a scene."

"But, Mother, it's the one to the file in Dad's study—"

"We still don't know that your father didn't take it."

The boys were reluctant to let the man go, but their mother's word was law. Breck then stalked out, slamming the front door behind him.

Mrs Hardy, still looking distressed, commented:

"I know you don't trust the man, Frank and Joe. But I hate to have a scene, especially since there was no proof against him."

"Sure, Mother, I understand," Frank answered. "Though the way he acted was mighty suspicious."

"I'll say," Joe agreed. "He'd better not show his face round here again."

The boys went upstairs, removed their football gear, and showered.

Five minutes later, while they were dressing, they heard Aunt Gertrude cry out. As the boys were speculating about what had happened, she knocked on their door.

"Hurry up! Go and find that man Breck. He's stolen your father's picture!"

Pulling on sweaters, they opened the door and followed her downstairs. Mrs Hardy was staring at the top of the baby grand piano where her husband's photograph had stood for nearly a year.

"I guess you were right after all about that salesman," she said. "He's taken Dad's picture. But why?"

"We'll find out!" Frank cried.

They raced from the house and down the street to their car. They had little hope of locating Breck, but to their relief Joe spotted him in the centre of town walking hurriedly along the sidewalk.

The convertible pulled up alongside him. As it came to a stop, he glanced at the boys, then started to run.

Leaping from the car, Frank and Joe gave chase. But Breck had a head start. He turned the corner. When the Hardys reached it, the man was not in sight!

·2·

A Clever Alibi

"Where did Breck go?" Joe cried, dismayed that their quarry had eluded them.

He and Frank glanced at both sides of the deserted street, seeing nothing but a few parked cars.

Suddenly Joe cried out. "Look, between those two parked cars. Isn't that a suitcase? And a man? Come on, Frank."

The boys dashed across the street. Joe approached the space between the cars from the sidewalk, Frank from the street.

"There he is! Grab him, Joe!" Frank exclaimed as Breck tried to make a getaway.

Joe, executing a perfect tackle, stopped the man dead in his tracks. Grunting and panting, Breck tried to shake him off, but Frank, coming up from behind, pinned the husky salesman's shoulders to the ground, while his brother clung grimly to his legs.

"Get off!" Breck cried, struggling to rise.

"Not until we've searched you," replied Frank, holding him even more tightly.

Just then Joe caught sight of a policeman sauntering along on the other side of the street.

THE CRISSCROSS SHADOW 17

"Hey, Casey!" he shouted to the officer, whom they had known for years. "We can use some help!"

Seeing the boys and their struggling captive, Casey broke into a run.

"What's up, fellows?" he cried as he reached them.

Frank and Joe released their grip on Breck, who now made no effort to break away.

"This man stole a picture of my father and the key to his filing cabinet," Frank replied, pointing to Breck, who glowered at the boys.

"Yes, we want him searched," Joe chimed in.

"All right," the officer's voice was stern. "Come along to headquarters, mister."

"Our car's round the corner," Frank said.

Breck started to object, but the policeman silenced him with a gesture.

"I never question Frank and Joe's judgment," he stated as they walked to the boys' convertible. "I guess you don't know that they're sons of the famous detective Fenton Hardy. And they're right smart detectives themselves. Solved lots of cases, they have. And not long ago they went out West and tangled with some real bad characters."

At police headquarters the group was met by Chief Ezra Collig, grizzled veteran of many a battle with Bayport's criminal elements. He and the Hardys had often worked together in rounding up underworld characters.

"Well, now, who's this man, boys?" the chief asked briskly. "What's he been up to?"

The Hardys quickly explained the mysterious activities of Breck.

"We can prove it, too!" Joe exclaimed, referring to the thefts of the picture and key. "All you've got to do is search him."

"No, you don't," Breck protested. "I insist upon calling my lawyer. You've got to permit that. I know my rights," he added threateningly.

"Okay," the officer agreed. "Who's your lawyer?"

"Miles Kamp," Breck replied quickly.

"Miles Kamp, eh? I've never heard of him. Must be a stranger to Bayport."

Frank and Joe looked at Breck suspiciously as the man dialled the phone on the chief's desk. After a few guarded words to Kamp, he hung up, a look of satisfaction on his face.

Ten minutes later Miles Kamp strode into the chief's office. He was a short, heavy-jowled man with a wide thin-lipped mouth that suggested a nasty streak in his character. He peered at them near-sightedly through thick-lensed glasses.

Frank turned to Joe. "I don't like his looks, do you?" he whispered as the salesman shook hands with the lawyer.

"No," the younger Hardy replied. "He looks even more suspicious than Breck."

"Now, what's going on here?" the lawyer said in an annoyed voice. "Why are you holding my client?"

"Calm down, Mr Kamp," Chief Collig said to him sternly. "Mr Breck is accused of stealing a key and a photograph belonging to Fenton Hardy. These are his sons, and they want this man searched."

"Searched? Why, certainly, my client will gladly agree to this," Kamp replied pompously. "Mr Breck," he said, turning to the leather-goods salesman whose face wore a smug look, "I advise you to let the police search you. We know you have nothing to fear."

At Chief Collig's order the policeman went to work. He turned Breck's pockets inside out and made him remove his shoes. Then he looked through the man's suitcase.

"Nothing suspicious here, boys," he reported.

Frank's eyes were intent on a bulge under the man's shirt. "What are you hiding there?" he asked.

The policeman investigated and found a framed photograph of Fenton Hardy.

"What was the idea of taking that?" Joe said accusingly.

Breck's face began to redden. "Well ... well, you see ..." the salesman stammered in embarrassment. "You're right. I *did* take your father's picture, and I apologize," he confessed sheepishly. "But I can explain."

"You'd better have a good reason," the chief interrupted.

"You see, I've always been a great admirer of Fenton Hardy," Breck went on rapidly, "and I've followed his exploits for years. So today, when I saw his picture on the piano, I couldn't resist picking it up as a souvenir."

"Well, that puts things in a somewhat different light," said Chief Collig.

"I knew you'd understand," Breck continued hastily. "And I hope the boys do. I'd like to keep the photo. It would mean a lot to me." There was a note of sincerity in his voice.

"I don't know," Joe replied slowly, looking at his brother questioningly.

"Please let me have it," Breck pleaded. "I'll give you back the frame. All I want is the photograph of Mr Hardy."

"Humph—" Chief Collig began, as all looked to him for advice. "The picture isn't autographed, is it?" he asked, scanning the photograph.

"No."

"Well," the officer continued soberly, "as long as it's not signed, and since Fenton Hardy's picture has appeared so frequently in newspapers anyway, I don't see what harm there'd be if this man keeps it. Since Mr Breck didn't take the key, we have no special charge to hold him. But it's up to you boys to decide, of course," he concluded.

Breck turned to Frank and Joe, a hopeful expression on his face. There were several moments of silence, during which Miles Kamp pulled out a handkerchief and made a great show of polishing his glasses. All eyes turned to the Hardys.

The boys looked at each other again. Years of working closely together had given each one the uncanny ability to know at a glance what the other was thinking.

Frank spoke. "I guess it's all right for him to keep the picture, as long as he's such a great admirer of Dad."

"All right. He can have it," Joe agreed. "I don't think Mother would mind."

"Thank you, thank you. I can't tell you how happy this makes me. It's very generous of you," Breck said effusively.

He moved impulsively to grasp the hands of the

Hardy boys to show his gratitude. Frank and Joe acknowledged his thanks coolly, their dislike of the man by no means lessened.

"Well, Chief Collig," Kamp interrupted in his pompous voice, "are you satisfied that my client has done nothing wrong? If so, I suggest you release him immediately."

"All right, you can go," the officer replied. Then he added sternly, eyeing the salesman with disfavour, "But I'm warning you, Breck, in the future you'd better not be helping yourself to pictures in people's houses."

"Thank you, Chief Collig," Kamp said unctuously. "We appreciate your co-operation. Good day, boys."

With a bow he strutted from the room, Breck at his heels.

"Breck won this round," remarked Frank. "But I still don't put any stock in his explanations."

"I know what you mean," agreed Collig. "We don't have a thing to hold him on, though."

A little while later, driving home in the convertible, Joe turned to Frank.

"Did you notice the back of Breck's hand as he was packing his suitcase?" he asked.

"Yes," Frank replied. "He had a strange-looking scar on the back of it in the shape of a W. You couldn't miss it."

"If he were a thief, it sure would be easy to spot him," Joe replied. "By the way, remember what Aunt Gertrude said about having seen his picture somewhere identifying him as a criminal?"

"That's right. We'll have to check with her on that."

Reaching home, the boys hurried up the steps. They

were famished and were looking forward to a delicious steak dinner.

"Hope Aunt Gertrude has apple pie to go with it." Joe grinned, anticipating the tasty meal that had been promised.

"I could eat at least two helpings," declared Frank as they entered the hall.

There they found Aunt Gertrude, greatly agitated. She was waiting for them.

"Joe! Frank! I was right about that so-called salesman all the time!"

"You mean about having seen his picture somewhere?" Frank asked.

"No, not that. But I just called Mrs Wilson, the one whose name was on the reference Breck showed us."

"Yes?"

"Just as I suspected," their aunt said triumphantly. "Mrs Wilson said that she had never heard of the man in her life. That reference was forged!"

A Dangerous Visit

"WHAT!" Frank cried out. "Mrs Wilson never heard of Breck?"

Aunt Gertrude shook her head.

"Then he forged the signature," Joe added. "Well, we sure were taken in. That guy probably had the key all the time—in his mouth maybe."

"And slipped it to Kamp. Joe, how could we have been so dumb?"

"Anyway, we can try to find him. I want to question him further."

"Not until we get a new lock for Dad's file," Frank said emphatically. "After going to all that trouble to get the key, Breck might try to use it!"

The boys excused themselves and hurried to a trusted locksmith with whom their father dealt. He supplied them with a new lock and instructed them how to install it.

After Frank and Joe had arrived home and had just replaced the old lock, a voice behind them said:

"Neat job, fellows!"

The boys whirled. "Sam Radley!" they exclaimed, and hurried across the room to greet their visitor.

Radley was Fenton Hardy's able assistant, and the

boys knew him well because he had helped them solve many tough problems. They had not seen him for several weeks and knew that he had been on the top-secret assignment with their father. They hoped he had news of Mr Hardy.

"You'll stay for dinner, Sam?" Mrs Hardy invited, coming into the room. "That will give us a chance to hear about your case."

"Thank you. I'd like to."

"How's Dad?" Joe asked after they sat down.

Sam smiled. "Your father's fine."

"What's the case about?" Frank put in. "Or can't you tell us?"

"Just a little," the detective replied, choosing his words carefully. "Your dad and I are working for the government. There have been several cases of sabotage in important industries throughout the country.

"It looks as though these cases are part of some master plan. We think the same gang is involved in all of them. But so far we haven't been able to find any clues that point to the guilty persons. That's about all I can tell you," Sam concluded.

Frank gave a long, low whistle. "Sounds like an important—and dangerous—case."

"We're working on a mystery of our own," put in Joe.

Briefly the boys recounted the events of the past few hours, ending with Aunt Gertrude's report of the forged letter of reference.

"That man Breck!" their aunt exclaimed. "I just know I've seen his picture in connection with something dishonest. Land sakes, I've been around detectives long enough to know a suspicious character when I see one!"

"You're better at it than I am," Mrs Hardy remarked ruefully. "But then, you're Fenton's sister."

"And just the person to help us find Breck," Frank said. "We'll go to police headquarters in the morning and look at their rogues' gallery."

Right after breakfast the next day the boys drove her downtown. She marched purposefully into headquarters, followed by her nephews. It was obvious that Aunt Gertrude meant to find out where she had seen the thief's picture. The boys knew that it was wise to keep in the background when she was in that mood.

"Good morning, Chief," she greeted Collig as the trio was ushered into his office.

"Aunt Gertrude wants to look at your mug file to see if she can identify Breck," Frank informed the officer.

"Well, well, so they're making a detective out of you, too," he joked, showing Aunt Gertrude several albums of pictures which lay on a table.

Miss Hardy leafed through the pages slowly. Suddenly she gave a start. "That looks as if it might be Breck," she said excitedly.

"It might be," replied Joe, peering over her shoulder, "except that it's Jerry 'the Character' Slocomb, and he's now serving time in the federal penitentiary for counterfeiting."

"Gracious sakes," responded Aunt Gertrude. "Well, what about him?" she asked, pointing to another photograph. "He certainly looks like Breck."

"Yes, he does," admitted Frank, "but that man was picked up a couple of days ago on the West

Coast for forgery. That's 'Fancy Fingers' Finley."

Collig laughed. "Miss Hardy, you've got to do better than that."

"I'll find him yet," Aunt Gertrude said with determination.

"Maybe if you come along with us to find him—" Joe suggested half-jokingly.

"And don't think I wouldn't capture him if I did!" she retorted. "Just the same, good detectives can stay right at home and solve certain mysteries. They don't have to gallivant all over the countryside."

For the next hour she pored over the pictures. Every once in a while she would pause at one which resembled Breck. Finally she closed the last album with a sigh of disappointment.

"He's just not here," Aunt Gertrude said dejectedly. "But I know I've seen his picture somewhere," she vowed.

"Maybe he was in disguise, Aunt Gertrude," Joe suggested. He was disappointed, too, that she had not been able to put her finger on a photograph of the mysterious man, and neither he nor Frank could find him.

After telling Collig of the man's forgery, Frank asked for Breck's address.

"We'd better work quickly before he decides to leave town," Frank said.

The officer consulted his files for a moment. "Breck's registered at the Excelsior Hotel," he informed them, mentioning the name of a third-rate hotel in the waterfront section of Bayport.

After dropping off Aunt Gertrude, who wanted

to do some shopping, the boys drove to the Excelsior.

"Have you a man named Wylie Breck staying here?" Frank asked the clerk.

The man consulted the register. "We did," he replied after a moment, "but he checked out."

The young detectives looked at each other in disappointment.

"I know," said Frank. "Let's phone his lawyer, Miles Kamp. Maybe he can tell us where Breck is."

The boys hurried to a telephone booth. After a few moments, Kamp answered.

"Yes, this is Miles Kamp," came the familiar pompous voice. "May I be of service to you?"

Frank asked where he could find Breck.

"I'm dreadfully sorry, my boy, but I can't help you at all. I haven't the vaguest idea where he went."

As Frank hung up, he wondered if this were true. "No help from that source," he said to Joe in disgust.

As they passed the desk again, the clerk beckoned to them. They hurried over.

"Aren't you Frank and Joe Hardy?" the man asked.

The boys admitted that they were.

"I thought so," the clerk continued in a low tone. "I recognized you from your newspaper pictures. I didn't care much for that guy Breck. If you're tracking him down, I'll let you look through his room for any possible clues. Follow me."

"Thanks," Frank said.

A minute later the clerk let them into the vacant room, then started back downstairs.

The boys searched thoroughly, looking into drawers, the wastebasket, even under the mattress, but found nothing that might help them locate the mysterious leather-goods salesman.

"Looks as if we're stuck," Joe said dejectedly as they came out of the room.

"Maybe not. There's a chambermaid. Let's see if she knows anything about Breck," Frank suggested when he saw a woman coming down the corridor carrying a pile of linen.

The boys approached her and Frank explained that they were looking for some trace of Breck.

"Breck, Breck," repeated the woman slowly. "Seems like I recall the feller. Hard-looking type. Shooed me out of the room once. Acted very strange."

Suddenly her face lit up. "I do remember something!" she exclaimed. "A bit of brown wrapping paper."

Going to a closet, she began to dig through a pile of trash. Presently the chambermaid gave a triumphant cry.

"Here it is!" she called. "I emptied this out of Breck's room."

The boys scanned the paper hurriedly.

"I can make out a name! Philip York!" Frank exclaimed. "But the address is blurred!"

"Philip York," his brother repeated. "I wonder if he could be a friend of Breck."

Taking the paper to a window, Frank held it to let the light strike it obliquely. In this way, he had often deciphered smeared or smudged writing.

"I've got it," Frank went on, reading haltingly. "Twenty-four Dock Street, Southport," he concluded triumphantly.

The address was that of a town several miles from Bayport on Eagle Bay, where the boys had often gone cruising.

"Come on, Frank!" Joe urged excitedly. "Let's go and call on this Philip York!"

Within half an hour Frank was guiding their convertible through the crowded streets of the grimy waterfront section of Southport. Reaching Dock Street, Joe began to look at the house numbers.

"There it is!" he exclaimed. "Pull up, Frank."

Twenty-four Dock Street was a ramshackle tenement. As the boys walked through the open front door, a stocky man dressed in dirty work clothes brushed rudely by them into the hallway.

"Frank," Joe whispered, "he might be York."

With a bound, the boys followed the man up the rickety stairs.

"Say, mister," Joe called out, "we want to ask you some questions."

The man turned round and faced them. "Who do you think you're following?" he demanded angrily.

"We want some information," Frank said boldly.

"So you want info, do you?" the man replied. "Well, who are you and what's your business here? Get out of here before I throw you out." He raised his arm in a threatening motion.

Undaunted, the boys held their ground.

"You'll throw nobody out," Frank said in a quiet but determined voice. "Do you know a Wylie Breck?"

"No."

"Are you Philip York?"

The man surveyed the boys standing shoulder to

shoulder. "No, I'm not," he answered. "What's the racket?"

Frank shrugged. "We heard they lived here. Thought we'd look 'em up."

"Oh, that's different. Well, I never heard of Wylie Breck, but there's a Philip York on the first floor," the stranger went on, somewhat calmed down.

The man pointed down the stairs. "He lives in that apartment. But I advise you kids to scram. You don't belong here. You'll get into trouble." He went up the stairs without explaining further.

Frank and Joe descended the stairs. The hallway was dark and had a musty odour. They rapped on the door of York's apartment.

After a few moments' wait they heard footsteps approaching the door.

"Get set, Frank, in case it's Breck and he slams the door in our faces," Joe whispered.

As the door was flung open the boys tensed themselves.

"What do you want?" An unshaven man, wearing a royal-blue sweater, challenged them. He was not Breck.

"We're looking for Wylie Breck and Philip York," Frank replied quickly, edging closer to the door.

"Breck? York?" the man rasped in a foggy voice. "Never heard of 'em. What business you got in this place, anyway?" he asked.

"We want to talk to them, that's all," Frank replied. "Maybe you've seen Breck around."

Frank described Breck, adding that he carried a suitcase full of leather goods.

"Never saw him," the man said.

Suddenly he raised his eyes and looked beyond the boys. Alert to danger, the boys turned.

As the door slammed behind them, they saw two dark shapes coming swiftly towards them.

"Look out!" Joe cried out.

·4·

The Telltale Moccasin

THE Hardys had only half turned to meet the attack when the two men crashed into them, chest-high. Joe was knocked out, Frank stunned.

Frank instinctively lashed out at the men with both fists. One of the attackers sank to his knees, but the other thug, coming from behind, got a stranglehold on the boy which rendered him helpless.

The Hardys' assailants dragged them down the hallway, pushed them into a closet, and locked the door.

"Leave the key in," a voice ordered.

It was several seconds before Joe regained his senses and remembered what had happened.

"Who could those guys have been?" Frank rammed his body against the door in an attempt to open it.

"Beats me. Let's try pounding first," Joe advised. "We don't want to pay for a broken door."

They thumped on the panel and waited. All was still. Then they began yelling:

"Help! Help!"

Presently they heard heavy footsteps coming down the hall. Was he friend or foe?

"I'm going to tackle him whoever he is," Joe said.

Before Frank could warn against it, the door opened and Joe charged the man outside. The two of them rolled on the floor in a heap.

"I've got him, Frank!" Joe yelled.

"Hey, lay off, fellows!" a familiar voice shouted.

"Chet Morton!" Frank exclaimed, recognizing their friend and helping him to his feet.

"Chet, how the dickens did you get here?" Joe demanded. "Gee, I'm sorry. I thought you might be one of the thugs who threw us in the closet."

"Hm!" said Chet as he dusted himself off. "I thought you would get in trouble, so I followed you from Bayport. My jalopy can't go as fast as yours. I nearly lost you, but a kid on the corner told me where you went."

"Good thing you came, Chet," Joe replied. "Sorry I was rough with you."

"That's okay," Chet said lightly. "Centres ought to be ready for surprise tackles."

"Let's talk again to that fellow in the blue sweater," Frank proposed. "Maybe he knows who hit us."

The trio hurried down the corridor, and Joe rapped on the door. No one answered. He pounded.

"Mighty mysterious," Frank commented. "That fellow knew we were in trouble. If he isn't in league with them, why didn't he help us out?"

"He must be a friend of Breck," Joe replied. "And that's why he didn't tell us that he was Philip York."

No one came to open the door. Either the man had gone out, or for reasons of his own would not answer.

"Let's report this whole business to the Southport police," said Frank. "There's nothing more we can do here."

"Now you're talking," agreed Chet. "This is a good place to stay away from."

After they had made a full statement at headquarters, and asked the sergeant to report any developments to Chief Collig, the boys drove back to Bayport.

Frank and Joe were puzzled by the day's events, but their determination to find Breck was stronger than ever.

Arriving home, they were greeted by their mother.

"Come on, boys," she said. "Hurry and wash. We'll eat in a few minutes."

After dinner, which included a second helping of chocolate walnut cake, Frank said:

"Joe, I have an idea. Why don't we try tracking down the manufacturer of that key case Mother bought from Breck? In that way, perhaps we'll be able to find out who he really is."

"Good idea. Let's start now."

They went into their father's study, where Mrs Hardy had put the new key case. Joe turned it over carefully in his hand. There was no name on it.

"But here's something inside," he announced.

Imprinted on the leather, in a corner of the case, was an odd mark:

The boys gave a sigh of satisfaction.

"Now we've got something definite to go on," Frank

said, smiling. "Tomorrow we'll show it to a leather-goods dealer and ask him what manufacturer uses this mark."

After football practice the next afternoon, they hurried straight to the shop of their white-haired friend Mr Nobbly.

"We'd like to find out who made this," Frank explained, showing the key case. "Here's the imprint. Can you tell us who uses this trademark?"

Mr Nobbly examined the mark closely. He shook his head slowly. "Sorry, boys, I never saw nor heard of that mark in all my thirty-five years in this business."

"Then it's probably some private maker's?" Frank asked.

"No doubt. It's fine, hand-tooled work. But it would be like hunting for a penny in the mud of Barmet Bay to find him."

Frank looked at Joe in disappointment. Another clue gone up in smoke!

"Come on," Joe said. "We'll keep checking."

They thanked Mr Nobbly and left the shop. For the next few days the Hardys called at every possible place in their quest for the maker of the key case.

They went to all the leather-goods shops in Bayport and examined key cases, wallets, handbags, and luggage. They even checked with shoe stores. But no one had ever seen such a mark.

Finally the boys had to postpone their search and settle down to hard football practice. Saturday came with the big game against Hopkinsville.

Frank was gloomy as the team donned their uniforms in the locker room.

"I guess it's no use trying to trace that symbol," he said dejectedly to Joe, pulling on his jersey.

"Looks as if you're right," his brother replied. "Well, let's forget about it for a while. We have a game to play, and you know what a whale of a team Hopkinsville has this year."

As they trotted along the corridor of the field house, Frank spied a moccasin lying on the cement floor. Ordinarily he would not have done any more than kick it out of the way. But being interested now in everything made of leather he bent down and picked it up.

"Joe, look!" he exulted. "The telltale mark!"

"Sure enough," Joe cried. "I wonder who dropped this." He queried the members of his team as they came from the field house. None owned the moccasin.

"Must be someone from Hopkinsville," Frank mused. "We'll find out later."

He took it along to the bench. The warm-up period was over and they were waiting for the whistle when one of the Hopkinsville players ran by. He noticed Frank holding the moccasin.

"Say, what are you fellows doing with that?" he asked. "It belongs to one of our ends—George Parks."

"Where is he?" inquired Joe. "We want to ask him about this moccasin."

The Hopkinsville player pointed. "He's the tall guy there."

At that moment the referee blew his whistle, signalling that the game was to begin.

The biggest crowd in years had gathered to watch the contest. Hopkinsville won the toss and elected to defend the north goal with the wind at their backs. Frank and Joe waited tensely in their positions as the Hopkinsville booter carefully placed the ball for the kickoff.

"Here it comes!" Frank cried. "Joe, it's headed right for you!"

Joe caught the end-over-end kickoff on the ten-yard line. Twisting and dodging, he carried the ball to mid-field. The Bayport stands cheered loudly.

Frank gained a couple of yards on the next play on a smash-through tackle. Then, on the following play, Joe faded back and tossed a short pass to the left end, Tony Prito. The dark-haired, wiry youth, a close friend of the Hardys, took the ball for a first down on the Hopkinsville thirty-five.

A couple of line bucks by Biff Hooper, another of their special friends, gained a few yards, and finally on the fourth down Joe faded back for a long pass.

Frank shot down the field like a streak of lightning, the ball sailing straight towards him. But just as he was reaching for it, a Hopkinsville player batted it down, and the opponents took over.

Frank moved along behind his linemen, grunting words of confidence to each in turn.

But in three plays Hopkinsville was on the Bayport four!

"This is the big one," Frank thought. "We've got to hold. This is the time to call up the secret defensive play we've been practising all week."

As the teams lined up for fourth down, Frank called out crisply:

"86X!"

Both Bayport tackles, instead of making the usual defensive charge, remained fixed in their positions and let the offensive linemen come to them. Through the tiny space created by this forward motion, Chet and Frank knifed into the enemy backfield and made havoc of the play, Chet making the tackle and stopping Newman, the Hopkinsville ace, in his tracks. The secret play had worked! The threat was halted! The remainder of the period was chiefly a punting duel between Frank and Newman. Each would run two ground plays and then punt. After several such exchanges, it became clear that Frank was getting more yardage with his high booming kicks that spiralled deep into enemy territory every time.

The Hopkinsville coach changed his strategy. He called a fresh end off the bench, briefed him with an arm round his thick shoulders, and sent him into the game. The team seemed to get new life as he came trotting on. This meant their favourite pass play!

Joe, just before he dropped back to his safety zone, got a quick glimpse of the replacement. He recognized him as George Parks!

"Now I'll be able to find out about the moccasin," Joe thought, but his excitement was lost in the barking of signals by the Hopkinsville quarterback.

Parks drifted down-field, got by Chet, and was lengthening his stride to take a long pass over his right shoulder, when Joe came racing across and knocked the ball right off his fingertips.

Joe ran back a few steps to pick up the ball. Tossing it to the referee, he turned quickly to talk to George Parks about the moccasin. But Parks had left the game and was almost off the field! He had been sent in for one play and that was all.

The first half ended in a scoreless tie. Each team went directly to its locker room.

As the Hardys came running side by side on to the field for the second half, Frank whispered to Joe, "We'll speak to Parks right after the game. That moccasin is a vital clue."

After the half-time interval Joe fastened his headgear a little more securely, took a reassuring look at George Parks on the Hopkinsville bench, and signalled for the kickoff.

The second half was a seesaw affair, with each team getting breaks and losing them.

With seconds to go in the last quarter, the Hopkinsville team suddenly fanned out in a widespread formation. Bayport shifted with them. Newman called his signals. Suddenly Joe noticed that Chet had not shifted. He was standing with a dazed look on his face. Then it dawned on Joe!

Each pass had been made into Chet's zone. He must have been hurt on that line smash. No doubt Newman would be throwing in there again!

The ball was snapped to Newman. He began to fade way back. He threw a long, lazy pass that soared over Chet's head towards the Bayport goal line.

The timekeeper's gun sounded as the ball was in flight. As soon as the ball was dead, the game would be officially over!

Joe, who had anticipated the play, was at the goal line, a step ahead of the Bayport pass receiver. He leaped up, wrenched the ball out of the grasp of his opponent, whirled, and scooted across the field, just outside of his own goal line.

At the fifty-yard line Frank threw a vicious block at the fastest enemy tackler, and Joe sprinted into the clear, with the wild uproar of the Bayport stands in his ears, straight down the sideline to the Hopkinsville goal.

The score was Bayport 6, Hopkinsville 0! Pandemonium reigned!

As Frank sent the ball straight through the crossbars, the gun sounded the end of the game.

Bayport had won 7-0 on Joe Hardy's one-hundred-yard dash for a touchdown! Frank hugged his brother, delirious with joy.

"What a run! There's never been a touchdown run that long in the history of Bayport High!"

"Yea, Hardy boys!" the Bayport fans shouted as they poured on to the field.

With cheers and singing, Frank and Joe were borne off the field on the shoulders of their team-mates. When at last they were set down, more fans crowded round to pummel the boys and shake their hands.

"Joe! Joe!" Frank shouted over the tumult. "We must see George Parks before he gets away!"

But the boys were trapped by their admirers as the Hopkinsville team dejectedly disappeared from the field. Fifteen minutes went by. But finally the Hardys broke loose.

They raced towards the parking lot, but when they reached it, they saw the Hopkinsville bus pulling out!

· 5 ·

Buried Treasure

FRANK and Joe gave chase, but it was too late. In a cloud of dust, the bus disappeared down the road, leaving the young detectives panting in the roadway.

As they trudged back towards the field house, Joe said, "I wonder what Parks did about his moccasin. It was still under our bench a few minutes ago."

The boys retrieved it.

"What do you say we return this to him tomorrow?" Frank asked.

"You bet."

They would have driven over that evening, but there was a school dance. Chet's attractive dark-haired sister Iola was going with Joe, and pretty blonde Callie Shaw with Frank.

Sunday afternoon the boys looked up Parks's address in the telephone directory, then drove to Hopkinsville.

"There's the house, Frank," Joe called out as they came to a tree-shaded ranch-style dwelling.

The tall, good-looking ballplayer answered the door.

"Hello, George," Joe greeted him.

"Joe and Frank Hardy!" the boy replied. "Come on in. Say, I'll never forget you fellows after yesterday's game."

"It sure was close," Frank said.

"What brings you to Hopkinsville?"

"We're returning some of your property." Frank held out a bag containing the moccasin.

"Thanks," Parks said, after Frank had explained about finding the shoe. "I hated to lose that. Those loafers are the most comfortable shoes I own. I had to wear my football shoes home."

Taking off their overcoats, Frank and Joe quickly outlined their special reason for coming and pointed to the R mark inside the moccasin.

"What we want to know," said Frank, "is where you bought them."

"Golly," George replied quickly, "I know where *I* got them, but I can't tell you where they were purchased."

"You didn't buy them yourself?" Joe asked.

"No. My uncle gave them to me as a present for my birthday last spring. All I know is that the moccasins were made by an Indian tribe. But what tribe I couldn't tell you," he concluded.

"Could you find out, George? It's important. It may help to catch a thief!"

"Good grief!" Parks exclaimed. "That's right. You fellows are detectives, aren't you? Well, my uncle lives a couple of blocks from here. I'll ask him."

He went to the phone, but the line was engaged, so he suggested that they walk over. His uncle Ben was intrigued by the Hardys' story of their quest for the maker of the leather goods.

"I remember those moccasins well," he said, drawing on his pipe. "I bought them from a stranger on a train. I never saw him before, and I've never seen him since."

"An Indian?" Frank asked.

"No."

"Did he mention the name of the tribe?"

Uncle Ben shook his head. "No, he didn't—just said he'd bought them from an Indian and that they were too small for him."

The Hardys thanked Mr Parks and George and started back to Bayport.

"It looks as though we're up a blind alley again. All our clues lead us nowhere," Frank muttered.

"You know," his brother said thoughtfully, "if that mark means anything, the name of the tribe may begin with an R. Maybe we ought to do some research on Indians."

"Good idea," Frank agreed. "I wonder," he added thoughtfully, "if Breck can be an Indian."

"He didn't look like a full-blooded one."

"No, I meant a half-breed."

"I'll settle for a quarter."

Presently a familiar house came into view.

"Let's stop at the Mortons'," Joe suggested. "I'm getting hungry, anyway."

Chet and Iola were home. Iola was mixing a batch of waffles under her brother's direction.

"We're just in time," Joe grinned. "Hope you've got plenty."

"Sure," Chet answered. "Iola, make twice as much batter. That'll be enough for a starter."

"I don't know about that," his sister replied teasingly. "Perhaps I'd better mix three times as much."

The chunky football centre was known for his appetite, and despite needling from his friends, never reduced his intake of food.

Supper was a jolly affair, but eventually the talk got round to the mystery of Wylie Breck. Frank told of the slim clue they had picked up from Mr Parks.

He concluded the story by telling them that the moccasin had been made by an Indian tribe. As he was saying, "If only we knew the name of a tribe that begins with R," Iola and Chet looked at each other strangely.

"You know of one?" Joe asked.

"N-no," Chet replied, and in a moment disappeared from the room.

The Hardys continued to eat waffles with syrup.

As Joe got up to get more butter from the refrigerator, he gave a strangled cry. Frank turned to see what had startled him.

Standing in the doorway was an Indian in battle regalia!

He raised his hand commandingly. Then a deep but strangely familiar voice intoned: "I am Chief Walla-patookunk."

"Chet!" whooped the Hardys, roaring with laughter as they recognized their buddy.

"Where in the world did you get that outfit?" Frank asked.

Chet himself was struggling to maintain a dignified and fierce look.

"This Indian warrior's suit," he replied solemnly. "Chief say you his prisoners." He pointed to Iola. "Bring um white girl to Wallapatookunk."

Iola now was giggling but pretended to be alarmed and shrank towards Joe.

"I will defend this maiden to the last arrow!" Joe

said, then added, "Have a heart, Chet, before I die laughing. Where did you get that Indian costume?"

"It's this way, fellows," Chet began, pulling out a handkerchief and wiping some of the red, black, and white crayon from his face. "My great-grandfather was a member of the Pashunk tribe."

"What!" Frank cried.

"Honest Injun," Chet insisted, "my great-grandfather belonged to the Pashunk tribe."

"He's right," Iola chimed in.

"Great-grandfather Ezekiel Morton was honorary Chief Wallapatookunk of the Pashunks. This getup I'm wearing is a ceremonial outfit used only on special occasions. It's been in our family for generations, and I just thought of it again when you mentioned those Indian moccasins."

"What does Wallapatookunk mean?" Frank asked.

"Gee, fellows," Chet stammered, "you really don't want to know, do you?"

"We certainly do," Frank insisted.

"Well, it means 'Eat-a-Whole-Moose,'" Chet answered reluctantly.

"Boy, your great-grandfather must have had some appetite. Say, why didn't your folks call you Ezekiel?"

"Whoever heard of a centre called Ezekiel?" Chet countered, ignoring the gibe.

"We don't know exactly how our great-grandfather got the Indian name," Iola spoke up, "but we do know a very strange legend that he used to tell. It has been handed down in our family."

"What is it?" Joe asked eagerly.

"According to the legend, a fabulous treasure is

buried in the territory where the Pashunks used to live!"

"Buried treasure!" The Hardys whistled in amazement.

"Where?" Joe inquired.

"No one knows."

"But there must be some clue," Frank insisted.

"Yes," Chet assented. "The legend says the treasure is buried in a crisscross shadow!"

"The shadow of what?" Joe asked.

"That's what we don't know, but I sure wish we could find the treasure," Chet concluded.

Just then the doorbell rang and Iola excused herself to answer it.

"Hi, Frank! Hello, Joe! Chet! What in the world!" cried Callie Shaw as she saw the boy's costume and his multicoloured streaked face.

"Callie," Joe said solemnly, with a sweep of his arm, "let me present Great Chief Walla—er—anyhow, heap big wheel among Indians!"

Callie, though still puzzled, joined the outburst of laughter at Joe's introduction of the disguised Chet.

Then Frank brought her up to date on news in the Morton household and also what he and Joe had learned at Hopkinsville.

"You've really made progress in your detecting," Callie commented. "If you could only find out something further about that R imprint."

"Say, why don't we get out our collection of old Indian books, Chet?" Iola spoke up. "Maybe we'll find some tribes that begin with R."

"And then we'll check on whether they're the ones who do leatherwork," Frank added enthusiastically.

Iola excused herself and returned a few minutes later with an armload of old volumes.

Immediately all the young people started thumbing through the books, intently scanning the fine print. The pages were yellowed with age.

There were dozens of tribes that no longer existed—names that had meant so much in the early days of the country—Abnakis, Shawnees, Narragansetts, and others that reminded the Bayport High students of the exciting days of the early colonists.

"This tribe we're looking for is probably so small that it didn't even make history," remarked Joe, breaking the silence. Everyone nodded agreement, but kept on leafing the pages determinedly.

But there was not a single tribe that began with an R!

Finally it was time for the Hardys to start home, since they did not wish to break football training rules. Frank rode with Callie as far as her house, with Joe following, then transferred to the convertible.

"I guess we're at the end of the Indian trail with that moccasin," Joe remarked.

"We may still find the R tribe," Frank said more hopefully. "I'm not giving up yet."

"I'm with you on that score," Joe agreed as they turned the corner near the Hardy home.

Suddenly Frank gave a start and sat bolt upright. "Look!" he whispered excitedly. "Coming out of that window!"

Joe followed his brother's gaze to the second floor of the Hardy house. In the moonlight they could see a man climbing out!

Frank cut the engine and stopped at the kerb. The

boys leaped from the car and dashed up the driveway.

As they looked up again, the intruder was dropping to the roof of the kitchen porch. Then a cloud passed in front of the moon and hid the scene in darkness.

"Come on! He mustn't get away!" Joe cried.

The boys heard a thud on the ground, and reached the porch just as the moon broke through the clouds.

They could see no one!

In the second that the clouds had obscured the moon, the intruder had disappeared as if the earth had swallowed him up!

·6·

An Elusive Suspect

WHERE had the man who had climbed out of the upstairs window gone?

"Quick!" Joe said to his brother. "I'll circle this side of the house. You take the other."

Finding no one, they searched the neighbouring gardens. It was no use. The intruder had disappeared.

"Let's go inside and see if he took anything," Frank urged.

Noticing that several lights had been turned on upstairs, the boys dashed to the first floor.

"It's Frank and Joe," Frank called. "Are you all right, Mother?"

"Oh, boys, what a relief to see you!" Mrs Hardy cried as they reached the hall.

Aunt Gertrude stood menacingly, an umbrella clutched in her hand.

"We saw a man crawling out of the upstairs window," Frank told them.

"Then why didn't you catch him?" Aunt Gertrude bristled.

"We tried," Frank confessed, "but he got away."

"Did he steal anything?" Joe put in. "Did you see him?"

"See him?" Aunt Gertrude echoed with indignation.

"We saw him, and if I ever get that fellow, I'll give him the thrashing of his life."

"Aunt Gertrude and I came home from the films. When we got upstairs we heard a noise in your father's study," Mrs Hardy explained. "We looked in and saw a masked man. As soon as he spotted us, he dived for the window and climbed out."

"What was he doing?" Frank asked.

"He was standing in front of the filing cabinet with a key in his hand!"

The boys rushed into Mr Hardy's study and examined the file carefully. Apparently it had not been disturbed.

"Good thing we changed that lock," Joe said.

"Right. But the criminal might have forced it open." Frank turned to his mother and aunt. "I guess you frightened him off in time."

"I wonder what he was after," Joe pondered.

"It could be almost anything," Frank replied thoughtfully. "Let's fine-tooth-comb this room. Maybe the fellow left a clue that may help us track him down."

They examined the study from wall to wall but found nothing. As Joe leaned against the cabinet, a disappointed frown on his face, suddenly something caught his eye. Reaching down, he pulled at a bit of wool snagged on the corner of one drawer.

"We missed this," he said. "Oh boy! What a clue!"

Triumphantly he flashed a strand of royal-blue wool! "That man in the house in Southport! Remember? He was wearing a royal-blue sweater!"

"Correct." Frank beamed. "Now we're beginning to get somewhere on this case!"

"That proves Breck *did* take the key!" cried Joe.

"After he skipped Bayport, either he or his lawyer gave it to the man in the royal-blue sweater and he came here tonight."

"Maybe those two guys who slugged us in that Southport tenement house were Breck and Kamp!" Frank reasoned. "They were just arriving to give Mr Blue Sweater the key."

"Everything ties together." Joe nodded in satisfaction. "But the important question's still not answered. What did this gang want from Dad's file?"

"Let's go back to Southport tomorrow and call on that blue-sweater guy again," Frank proposed.

Since the football squad was excused from practice on Monday, the Hardys were able to start for Southport as soon as classes were over.

"How about coming along, Chet?" Frank asked as they got ready to leave.

"Sorry, fellows. I promised Dad I'd help around home. But listen, you two, don't get yourselves in the hospital. We've got a tough game to play on Saturday and—"

"Where're you going?" Tony Prito spoke up. "Maybe I can be your bodyguard."

"Swell."

The three boys drove to the dock where the Hardys' small powerboat the *Sleuth* was moored. They would make the trip to Southport by water.

When they arrived, Frank and Joe asked Tony to guard the *Sleuth* while they were gone. Then they headed up a steep cobblestoned alley to the street and walked into the main entrance of the tenement where Philip York lived.

Joe rapped on the apartment door while Frank kept an eye on the dim corridor to avoid another surprise attack.

The door was opened by the man they had come to see. He was wearing the telltale blue sweater.

"What do you want?" he asked roughly.

"To talk to you."

The man's eyes widened when he recognized his callers. "You boys are going to get hurt coming here," he said threateningly. "I can't give you any information."

"Oh no?" Joe retorted sceptically, then shot the question, "What were you doing in our house last night?"

"Your house? I've never been near the place in my life," York replied angrily.

"That's your story," Frank spoke up. "Here, take a look at this," he said, forcing his way in and suddenly confronting the man with the piece of blue yarn. "It came from that sweater you're wearing," he declared, pointing to a tear in the front of it.

The man looked blank, then recovered. "Maybe it did, maybe it didn't. Anyway, it ain't my sweater," he said defensively. "I borrowed it."

"We don't believe you," Frank answered firmly. Both boys were in the room now. "You'd better start talking."

"Look, fellows," York said meekly. "Take it easy on a guy that ain't to blame, will you? I'll do anything you ask. You've got the goods on me."

The Hardys had not expected to get a confession that easily. They looked at each other with satisfaction. At last they were making headway on the case!

"Come along to the police station with us," Frank said sternly. "They'll want to hear what you have to say."

"Okay," the man replied nervously. "I'll have to get my coat out of the bedroom. Wait here."

Before they could object, he turned, went into an adjoining room, and closed the door.

"We'd better keep a close watch on him," Frank advised. "He may try to get away."

Joe agreed, and called, "Say, you in there!"

There was no reply.

"Let's see what he's up to!" Joe exclaimed.

The boys burst through the door. Their eyes took in the shabbily furnished bedroom in a glance.

No one was in sight!

"There's no way out except by the windows and they're locked from the inside," Frank stated. "He's got to be here somewhere!"

They began a careful search of the room. When Frank crawled under the bed he found a trap door that opened downwards.

"Here's how he got out!" he exclaimed. "Joe, you guard the hall and I'll go after him this way."

"Okay. Give our whistle if you need me."

Frank squeezed through the opening on to a rope ladder which swung down from the edge of the trap door.

"This must be the basement," he told himself as he reached the end and stepped on to the floor.

He whipped out his pocket flashlight and flicked it on. He saw no one.

Inch by inch Frank went over the cellar. But the man in the royal-blue sweater was not there.

"How are you getting on?" Joe called down.

"He got out of here somehow." At that moment Frank heard a familiar sound—the *put-put* of a motor-boat.

"This basement must be very close to the dock!" he shouted up to Joe. "There's a door. I'll let you know what happens."

He hurried over, twisted the knob, and pushed. The door opened easily.

Blinking in the bright sunlight, Frank looked around. He was standing alone on a small dock that poked its nose into Eagle Bay.

Joe was peering from the living-room window. Now he raised the sash and called:

"See anything?"

"Nothing but the *Sleuth*."

Joe looked in the direction his brother was pointing.

"Tony! Hey, Tony!" Frank shouted across to the next dock.

Their friend's head appeared over the stern. "Hello. I'll come and get you."

"Did you see anybody walk out of here?" Frank called.

"Sure. A few minutes ago two men came out."

"Where'd they go?"

"They boarded a speedboat and headed off towards Bayport."

"Did one of them have on a blue sweater?"

"No. But come to think of it, one man had something blue rolled up under his arm."

"He's the guy we're looking for!" Frank exclaimed. "Joe, come on down! We're going after them!"

Tony brought the *Sleuth* up and the Hardys hopped in. Then the boat shot out into Eagle Bay and headed for Bayport.

Scanning the bay, his hand shading his eyes from the sun, Tony suddenly shouted, "There they are, Frank. Give 'er the gun!"

The other motorboat was ploughing through the choppy water at a fast clip. Frank turned on full speed and the *Sleuth* fairly leaped across the waves. Gradually it began to close up the distance that separated them.

"We're catching up!" Tony exulted.

In a few moments the boys could clearly see two figures in the stern and a third at the wheel.

"There's the fellow with the blue sweater, all right," Joe announced. "But he's masked now!"

"Say—the other one might be Breck," guessed Frank, gripping the wheel tensely.

"Could be," returned Joe. "He's got a mask on, too."

Relentlessly the *Sleuth* ploughed on, closer and closer to the fleeing craft. Finally Frank narrowed the gap and began to edge in towards the boat ahead.

"York's trying to hide!" yelled Joe as he discerned a figure hunched over in the rear seat. Just then the man beside York jerked his head round towards the pursuers and shouted something to the pilot of the fleeing speedboat.

Instantly the craft swerved sharply to the left. But just as swiftly Frank turned the *Sleuth*.

From then on it was a zigzag chase. The fugitive boat veered crazily from side to side. Nevertheless, the *Sleuth* clung to the course, and Tony shouted encouragingly:

"Atta boy, Frank! Stick to 'em!"

York's companion turned round. Standing up, he shouted back:

"Scram outta here, you fool kids!"

The man at the wheel now resumed a straight course, making a beeline for Bayport.

The *Sleuth* roared up behind the speedboat. Suddenly York's companion bent down. As he straightened up, he raised a heavy log of wood and heaved it. The log soared through the air, directly in the path of the onrushing *Sleuth*.

"Frank! Look out!" Joe cried.

Frank swung the wheel with all his might. But it was too late. With a splintering crash the *Sleuth* rammed the log!

·7·

A Lucky Break

THE shock of the collision was so violent that the boys were catapulted into the cold water of Eagle Bay.

In a few seconds three heads emerged from the waves.

"Joe! Tony!" Frank shouted out. "Are you all right?"

"Okay, here!" Joe called.

"I'm all right, too," Tony answered.

To their amazement the *Sleuth* was still afloat, drifting aimlessly some yards away. As the boys swam to it, they noticed than an immense hole had been torn in her bow at the waterline.

"She's going to sink!" Tony cried woefully.

They clambered aboard and Frank discovered that the impact had switched off the engine. He tried to start it, but it was dead!

"This is a fine pickle," he said in disgust.

"Where did the other boat go?" Tony asked.

The boys scanned the bay, but could see only a cluster of small craft near the shore. The men had made their escape!

"There's one clue, though, that they've given us," Frank put in. "Did you notice that huge scar on the fellow's hand before he tossed the log at us?"

"Say—that's right!" exclaimed Joe. "I did see it. It

was W-shaped, too! That means it was probably our friend Breck!"

"We practically had him!" Frank groaned. "Fine time to be stuck like this."

"And we're drifting with the tide," Tony pointed out as he noticed the shoreline receding.

Half an hour later he motioned towards a low-slung cabin cruiser that was bearing down on them.

"Look, fellows, isn't that the Coast Guard cutter *Mallimuk*?"

The three boys shouted and waved their arms to signal the cutter. The captain saw them and drew alongside. When Frank explained the reason for their predicament, Captain Barnes shook his head in anger.

"I'll send out an alarm for those men right away," he assured them. "Meanwhile, we'll give you a lift and some dry clothes."

While he radioed headquarters, a guardsman threw a line from the cutter. Joe fastened it to the *Sleuth*, and the craft was towed to its dock.

The boys thanked the men and went to their car. After dropping Tony off at his house, they made arrangements to have the boat repaired, then drove home. Mrs Hardy was waiting anxiously.

"Mother," Joe asked, "is something the matter?"

"Yes, there is," she replied. "It's Sam Radley. He's been injured!"

"What happened, Mother?" Frank asked. "One of the saboteurs get him?"

"Yes. Sam caught up with a suspect and they had a tussle. The man got away, but Sam was thrown and broke his leg."

"Where is he now?"

"In Bayport Hospital."

"We'd better go to see him right away," Frank declared.

The boys were at the hospital in a few moments. They found their father's associate with his left leg in a plaster cast.

"We're sorry about this," Joe said. "How do you feel now?"

"Pretty well, boys. But I sure hated to lose my man."

"What happened?" Frank asked.

Briefly, Sam Radley told them he had received a tip to look along the waterfront for certain characters and had trapped one of the suspects at a boathouse outside Bayport. While he was taking him to his car, the man had made a break for it. In the fracas that followed, the saboteur had pushed Sam into a deep ditch. The detective pointed to his cast.

"This was the result."

"At least you're making headway on the case," Joe remarked.

"I *was*." Sam smiled ruefully. "This sets me back. But without question your father and I are getting closer to cracking the case. On the other hand, the saboteurs are becoming bolder. They're likely to strike anywhere, any time!"

"Gosh," Joe said, "I hope you'll get them soon before they do any real damage." Then he asked, "Sam, what did the man who escaped look like?"

"He's heavy-set," the assistant detective replied. "Dark-haired and swarthy-complexioned."

Frank leaned forward tensely.

"Were there any distinguishing marks on this man that you tussled with?" he asked.

"Yes. He has a large W-shaped scar on the back of his right hand."

"Scar on the back of his hand!" Frank exclaimed, and told of their recent adventures. "The man who threw the log at our boat had a W-shaped scar on the back of his right hand. And what's more," he continued eagerly, "Breck, the phony leather-goods salesman, had the same scar on *his* hand. I'll bet that Breck, the man in the boat, and the saboteur are all the same person!"

"You're right," Joe agreed.

Sam Radley stroked his chin thoughtfully and looked down at his injured leg. "Maybe you'll catch him before I do. Keep your eyes open and your wits about you. Those fellows are dangerous. The one who got away from me is known as Killer Johnson."

"Was he hiding in the boathouse or had he just arrived there in a boat?" Joe asked.

"He was just coming out of the boathouse when I got there," Sam answered. "I didn't see a boat, though."

The boys talked a few moments more with Sam, then said good-bye, promising to watch for clues that might help on the sabotage case.

On the way home Joe said, "I wonder where that boat disappeared to after the log was thrown at us."

"There are a lot of little coves and inlets along the shore that it could have ducked into without being seen," his brother replied.

"Maybe we ought to look along the shore," Joe suggested.

After an hour of fruitless searching the boys turned homeward.

"Those fellows probably left town. They may have seen the Coast Guard pick us up. I'm sure that after they dropped Breck they went into hiding," Frank pointed out.

"I think our best bet right now is to follow up the clue of the moccasin," said Joe. "It's a clue to the real identity of Breck and might lead us to his pals."

When the boys arrived home they found dinner ready. During the meal they told their mother and Aunt Gertrude about Sam Radley's condition and their suspicion that he had been after the same man they were.

"I guess we'll have to do Sam's work," Frank observed with a sidewise look at his aunt, knowing she would object.

"Sam's work, indeed!" she cried out. "You leave the saboteurs to the big detectives!"

"Tall, you mean? I'm as tall as Sam."

"Now, boys," Mrs Hardy cautioned, hoping the banter would not get out of hand.

"Solving crimes certainly gives them a good appetite for food and wit," Aunt Gertrude declared as each was served a second helping of fricasséd chicken and dumplings.

When they finished, the young sleuths leaned back with a sigh.

"Aunt Gertrude," said Joe, "sometimes I'd rather eat one of your meals than solve a mystery!"

At that moment the telephone rang. Frank picked it up. It was Iola. "Callie and I have been looking through some more Indian books and we've come across something important."

"What is it?"

"We've found the name of an Indian tribe that begins with an R!"

Frank whistled in amazement. "Great work, Iola. What's the name?"

"The Ramapans."

"Ramapans?" Frank repeated. "Listen, we'll be right over."

Twenty minutes later the Hardys arrived at the Mortons.

"Iola and I decided to check some other books that Chet remembered were in the attic," Callie explained. "We'd just about given up our search when we came across the Ramapans."

"That's great," said Joe. "Where are they located and what are they like?"

He pulled out a notebook and pencil ready to take down all the information.

"Well, the Ramapans are a small tribe. They live on a reservation about five hundred miles from here," Callie replied.

"Yes. Go on," Frank urged eagerly as the girl paused.

"They are skilled in making small trinkets and leather articles."

"Skilled in leatherwork!" Frank exclaimed.

"I thought that would make you sit up and take notice." Chet grinned. "Just come to Morton and Company for the best in detecting."

"Can you show us on the map where the Ramapans live?" Frank asked.

Chet brought out an atlas and opened it. After turning several pages, he pointed.

"Here it is. Not many people live in this region."

The Hardys recognized the area as rugged territory made up mostly of mountains and forest.

"Say," Chet called out suddenly, "that's the area where the Pashunks used to live!" His face lit up with expectation. "Fellows," he said, "I have a wonderful idea. Let's go there and search for that buried treasure!"

"Sounds good, Chet," Frank replied. "But the Ramapans might not agree. They own the land where their reservation is located. And you've forgotten something else—school. How would you get time off from classes?"

"And even if we could, how about the football games?" Joe asked. "Bayport High might get along without Frank and me, but our big centre—no!"

Chet beamed at the compliment.

"Right now, we have a mystery to solve," Joe said.

"And we do have a good clue to the maker of the key case and the moccasin," Frank added.

The young people spent the rest of the evening poring over the story of the Ramapans, learning their history and customs. As the Hardys were leaving, Frank said:

"I certainly hope we can put all this knowledge to some good use."

The next afternoon, between the end of classes and football practice, he and Joe dropped in to see Police Chief Collig and ask if there was any news from the Southport police about Breck and the man in the blue sweater.

"Nothing good," the officer replied, leaning back in his swivel chair. "They've disappeared. An alarm has been sent out for them. Don't worry, boys," he went on encouragingly. "Those two will turn up again, and when they do, they'll be arrested."

Frank looked at his watch. "Well, it's time to get over to football practice. Thanks for the information, Chief."

During the next two hours they worked hard, under the watchful eye of Coach Devlin. Finally, when the sun was setting over the empty stands, he dismissed the squad.

The Hardys trotted to the showers side by side.

"You know," Joe said, "I'd like to follow up the key-case clue in the Ramapan country right away. We might fly up there for the weekend."

"That wouldn't be enough time to make a thorough investigation," his brother pointed out. "How about Christmas vacation?"

"Gosh, Frank, I'd hate to wait that long to call on the Ramapans. But maybe we'll figure out a way."

When they arrived at school the next morning, a crowd of boys and girls were gathered round the main entrance. The Hardys hurried up, curious to find out what was going on. Usually students lingered outside only briefly, then went to their classes. Seeing their friend Biff Hooper in the group, Frank and Joe walked over.

"Hi, Biff!" Frank greeted the rangy fullback. "What's all the excitement?"

"Have a look for yourself," Biff replied, pointing to a sign tacked on the entrance.

The boys edged over for a closer look, but knew from the animated conversations what it said.

"Because of a breakdown in the heating plant, all classes and sports have been suspended. You will be advised over the radio when school will reopen."

"Pretty neat, eh?" Biff said delightedly. "Now I'll have time to work on that sailing-boat I'm building for next summer."

Joe's face broke into a wide grin. "One guess, Frank, what we'll do with the time."

"Go up to the Ramapan country!"

"Right. Let's tell Chet. He'll probably want to come along and hunt for that buried treasure!"

Their stout friend, who never reached school until the very last minute, arrived at that moment in his rattling jalopy.

"What! No school! Do I want to go!" he exclaimed when he heard the news. "Yippee!"

·8·

A Desperate Attempt

"OKAY, Chet. Let's go to the station and find out about trains," Frank suggested.

The agent informed them that a through train for Lantern Junction, the nearest village to the Ramapans, stopped at Bayport at eleven o'clock.

"Don't be late!" Frank warned Chet as he dropped them at the house. "Remember, we don't have all day to make that train—just a couple of hours!"

"Say, whose treasure is this, anyway?" Chet called. "I'm practically at the station now!" And his ancient car lurched and clattered down the street.

Reaching home, Frank and Joe told their mother and Aunt Gertrude about the heating-plant break-down and their plan to visit the Ramapans.

Mrs Hardy was somewhat taken aback by their announcement of the proposed trip. But she resolved not to voice the anxiety she felt.

"Take plenty of warm clothes," she advised. "It's very cold up there at this time of year. And I'll get some money for you."

"If I were the school principal, I'd give you plenty of home work so that you couldn't go gallivanting!" Aunt Gertrude said.

"Zingo! I'm glad I never had you for a teacher, Auntie!" Joe cried.

He fled upstairs before she could reply, Frank following. They had barely started pulling out ski clothes when their aunt came into their room.

"Shoo!" she ordered. "I'll do the packing. Go and get your cases!"

"We will," Joe agreed cheerfully. "There's no better packer in Bayport."

At that moment Mrs Hardy entered the room. "Here's a letter for you," she said, handing it to Joe. "A boy brought it."

"Thanks, Mom." He studied the envelope for a moment.

"Who's it from?" Frank asked.

"I don't know," Joe replied. "There's no return address and the handwriting's not familiar." He ripped open the plain white envelope. As he read the message, his eyes widened in surprise. He gave the letter to his brother. Frank's eyebrows shot up at the warning it held:

Don't meddle. Stay home if you value your life. R.

"What is it?" Mrs Hardy asked.

"Yes, something mighty peculiar's going on, judging from the look on your faces," Aunt Gertrude added.

Frank read the note aloud. The women gasped, and instantly asked the boys to cancel the trip.

"But, Mother," Frank said, "I'm sure Dad would want us to carry through. If we told him someone was trying to get his secret papers and didn't follow it up, he wouldn't think much of us as detectives."

"Of course," Joe said, "if you and Aunt Gertrude are afraid to stay alone—"

"Such talk!" Their aunt bristled. "Didn't I chase that burglar away singlehanded?"

Finally, consent to the trip was given and the packing went on. Frank and Joe left the room. Out in the hall Frank whispered:

"I guess that Breck or York must have been spying on us and heard our plans."

"Yes, and those fellows really mean business."

Frank set his jaw. "Now that we know we're dealing with a gang that's desperate, it'll be all the more exciting tracking them. What do you say we take this note to Chief Collig and have it analysed for fingerprints, et cetera. We haven't time to do it ourselves."

"Okay. Let's get moving. We don't want to miss that train."

When the boys arrived at police headquarters, the desk sergeant greeted them. "Chief Collig's in his office. Go right in."

Frank handed over the letter and told the Chief about their coming trip.

"This is serious," Collig declared after reading the message. "I warn you boys to be on the alert every minute."

"We'll do that," Joe promised.

Pointing to the envelope, Frank asked, "Don't you think a lab check of this letter would be in order, Chief Collig?"

"Right you are, Frank. Come on. We'll do it right away," he replied, beckoning them towards the police department's crime laboratory.

A check of the fingerprints on the letter did not tally with those of any known criminal, and there were no identifying marks to tell from whom the letter had come.

"It's not a whole sheet, and it's written on heavy paper, we know that much," Chief Collig determined. "I'd say it was cut from a long, narrow sheet."

Frank picked up the letter. "I wonder—" he began slowly, "I wonder if it could be *legal* paper." He held one edge of it to the light. "Yes, it is!" he exclaimed, seeing the semblance of a blue line where the paper had been cut.

"Fine deduction, Frank," the chief complimented him. "But what person who uses legal paper might be mixed up in this business?"

"Miles Kamp!"

"Of course!" the officer agreed. "He's Wylie Breck's lawyer!"

Picking up his telephone, Chief Collig said, "Sergeant, I want two men detailed to watch Miles Kamp. Shadow him day and night and give me a full report on everything he does."

He replaced the instrument in its cradle and turned to the Hardys.

"I think we're getting somewhere at last, thanks to you. That note tipped the gang's hand." He looked at his watch. "Don't miss your train. And good luck," he called.

The boys stopped at the house just long enough to collect their cases and say good-bye to their mother and Aunt Gertrude.

The railway platform was crowded, but they had no trouble finding Chet among the throng. He was surrounded by enough luggage for a month.

"That's rugged country, and a fellow can't be too well equipped," Chet insisted.

The three made their way to the edge of the platform when they heard the whistle of the approaching train. Chet leaned over the track to try to look round a bend beyond the station.

"Here she comes, fellows!" he cried, catching a glimpse of the engine.

The train came closer. As it turned the bend, a shrill scream from the street cut the air.

At the instant that everyone's attention was diverted, the Hardys suddenly felt themselves shoved towards the track by strong hands. They struggled against the pressure but were thrown off balance.

"You will butt in where you have no business, will you?" a rasping voice muttered in Frank's ear.

"Stop!" Frank cried out.

But the plea was useless. Their arms flailing the air, both boys went tumbling off the platform directly into the path of the oncoming train!

·9·

Conflicting Reports

THE train bore down on the Hardys who were sprawled across the track. Men shouted. Women screamed and covered their eyes. Brakes shrieked.

Instinctively Frank rose and jumped back. But Joe was stunned, the breath knocked from him. Chet was the first onlooker to make a move. Quickly he leaped from the platform, lifted Joe, and hurled himself and his burden out of the path of the train.

"Oh! Thank goodness!" someone cried out.

Still trembling, Frank and Joe stood stock-still, unable to believe they had been saved. Then Joe looked at Chet and murmured:

"Thanks, pal."

As the train came to a stop, everyone excitedly began to talk at once. What had happened? Had the surge of the crowd pushed the boys on to the track?

"No," Frank answered, recovering his wits. "We were shoved."

Just then the conductor rushed up. After a brief explanation, Frank asked him to hold the train for a few minutes.

"I want to find the men who caused all the trouble," he said.

The conductor nodded, and announced:

"There will be a five-minute stop. All passengers for this train please remain on the platform."

The Hardys and Chet hurriedly asked persons on the platform whether anyone had seen the men responsible for pushing the boys on to the track. But none of the crowd had noticed anyone running away from the scene. They had been looking towards the street to see who had screamed.

"I guess it's no use," Frank declared. "Those guys have probably skipped out."

When the three boys were seated in the train, Chet remarked, "Do you think the person who screamed had anything to do with the shove?"

"Yes," Frank answered. "The whole setup was planned."

"The writer of that note meant business!" Joe exclaimed.

"What note?" Chet inquired. When he learned of the warning, he whistled and asked, "Who do you figure signed himself R?"

The Hardys shrugged, saying the initial most likely stood for Ramapan, but might have been borrowed by someone not connected with the tribe.

"Hm!" said Chet, cupping his face in his hands. "We may be running right into danger. Maybe—"

"You don't mean you want to go back and not look for the treasure!" Joe exclaimed in mock disgust.

"Well, not exactly, but you fellows have a habit of getting me into tight spots."

Frank said grimly, "Those platform pushers will have their hands full if they try to pull any more funny business."

"Let's forget about the mystery for a while and enjoy this trip," Chet interposed half an hour later.

"Okay," Joe replied. "I'll switch on the radio."

He snapped open the small portable set he was carrying and adjusted the dials to a programme of hit tunes.

As they sat watching the countryside speed by, they listened idly to various programmes. At last a newscast came on.

Suddenly Frank sat bolt upright. "Listen to that!" he exclaimed.

The announcer's voice came clearly.

"—serious case of sabotage in Chicago. An important government project has been bombed by saboteurs, leaving the place in ruins.

"Fenton Hardy, the famous investigator, is on the scene at this very moment. When interviewed, Mr Hardy said that he is following up scattered clues, but that so far none of the culprits has been captured. And now for news on the international front—"

Frank clicked off the set. "The gang has struck again!"

Chet's face wore a puzzled look. "I thought your dad was supposed to be in California. Now he turns up in Chicago."

"That is strange," Joe agreed, frowning. "He must have flown there in a big hurry."

"But I'm sure Mother just heard from him in California," Frank insisted. "As soon as the train arrives, we're supposed to call home. Let's ask her about it."

The train was now moving along more slowly, ascending the rugged mountainous country where the

Ramapan community was located. At last the big diesel pulled into Lantern Junction.

The Hardys and Chet were the first to alight and hurried to the telephone booths in the station. Joe put in a long-distance call to Bayport while Chet called a local hotel for reservations.

"Hello, Mother," Joe said. He decided not to mention the episode at the Bayport station. "Have you heard from Dad since we left?"

"Yes."

"There was a report on the radio," Joe went on, "that he's working on a sabotage case in Chicago. Is that right?"

As she was replying, Frank crowded into the booth with Joe. He could hear her answer plainly.

"I heard the report too. I'm baffled by the whole thing. Your father can't be in two places at once, and I've just had a wire from him. It was sent from California!"

Just then Chet sidled up to the boys. "We can stay at the Grand Hotel," he reported. Joe passed the news along to his mother, then said, "I guess there's nothing we can do about Dad. But keep us posted of any new developments."

"I will, and take care of yourselves."

"Okay. 'Bye now."

Despite the fact that Mrs Hardy did not seem concerned about her husband, Frank was uneasy.

"Let's call his hotel in San Francisco," he suggested. "That will clear up this whole business."

"Good idea," Joe replied. "But we should register at the Grand first."

As soon as they were in their room Frank gave the operator the call. When the connection was made, he said:

"I'd like to speak to Mr Fenton Hardy."

"One moment, please," the operator at the hotel replied.

Then a man's voice broke in. "Who is it you want?" he asked.

"Is Mr Fenton Hardy there?" Frank repeated, leaning close to the receiver. "This is his son, Frank Hardy."

"I can't tell you!" the man replied and hung up.

Frank replaced the receiver, frowning thoughtfully.

" 'Can't tell you,' " he echoed slowly, after telling Joe and Chet the strange reply.

"What did the man mean?" Chet asked, puzzled.

"I'd say the hotel actually doesn't know where Dad is," Joe answered.

"Or it could be that they're obeying instructions from Dad not to disclose where he is," Frank reflected.

The boys began unpacking in their neat but simply furnished quarters. Frank and Joe would bunk together, with Chet in the adjoining room.

"Boy, wouldn't I give anything to go hunting or fishing up here," Chet remarked. "But we have to find the treasure first."

"Not *we*," Joe corrected. "Frank and I came here to follow up the key-case clue."

"Have it your own way," Chet replied.

The three put on warm, sturdy attire for their hike through the woods to the Ramapan village, then went downstairs and asked the clerk for directions. They were told that the trail through thick woods to the isolated community, which lay miles from any habitation, was a rough one. The clerk strongly advised them not to attempt it until morning.

His words were not exaggerated, as the boys learned the next day. The trail to the Ramapans was narrow and twisting, making it necessary for them to walk single file. Occasionally the stillness of the forest was broken by the cry of an animal or the fluttering of a startled bird.

Eventually the boys found themselves in a small clearing. Pausing to catch their breath which made white clouds in the crisp air, they heard a crackling in the underbrush in the woods beyond.

Suddenly the branches on the other side of the clearing parted and an Indian stepped out to face them! No one spoke.

The man was wearing suède trousers and coat with fringes. Long, shiny black hair hung down over his shoulders.

He broke the silence. "No be afraid. I your friend," he addressed them in a strange accent.

"You're a Ramapan?" Frank asked him.

The stranger did not reply. Instead, he said:

"I give warning. You boys walk to bad country."

"What do you mean?" Joe demanded.

"You come to unfriendly tribe. Very dangerous people."

"Dangerous?" Frank said sceptically. "What's so dangerous about an Indian tribe these days?"

"You listen to warning, paleface," the man continued, anger in his tones. "Tribe guard deep secret. No want visitors."

With that he turned on his heel and disappeared among the trees. The boys looked at each other dumbfounded.

Chet paled. "S-a-a-y, fellows," he said shakily, "maybe we'd better take his advice and turn back."

"Not on your life," Joe replied determinedly.

Frank agreed, adding, "I'll bet that fellow isn't even a member of the tribe. That accent he had was too thick. No real Indian talks like that these days. I'm sure he's a phony."

"You mean he faked everything—the Indian rig and the accent?" Chet demanded.

"Sure."

"Then who is he?"

"One of the gang we're trying to track down."

"You're right, Frank!" Joe exclaimed. "Quick! Before he gets away, let's follow him!"

-10-

Tom-toms

THE boys crashed through the thick brush in pursuit of the strange Indian.

"Where'd he go?" Chet puffed.

"Here are some fresh footprints!" Frank exclaimed. "Come on!"

They raced along, following the tracks Frank had observed. The narrow, rocky path wound deeper into the dim, silent forest.

The trail suddenly twisted sharply to the right. Frank, still in the lead, held up his hand, signalling a halt.

The trio stood still, looking intently for any indication of which way the man had gone. They came to the conclusion that he had jumped from stone to stone, losing his pursuers completely.

"We may as well continue on to the Ramapan village after we have a snack," Frank decided.

The boys quickly ate sandwiches they had brought along and drank from a sparkling mountain spring.

As they set off again, Chet cried out tensely: "Listen!"

The Hardys paused. The sound that came to them was a muffled, regular beat.

"Tom-toms!" Frank exclaimed.

Chet turned pale and looked nervously about him. "S-a-a-a-y, fe-l-l-ows, those tom-toms—maybe that man we just met was right. What if those Indians are getting ready to attack us!"

Frank and Joe broke into laughter.

"Aren't you young Chief Wallapatookunk?"

Chet blushed furiously. "Come on," he said with a sudden show of bravery. "Let's go."

They moved along another quarter of a mile without disturbance. Then a fawn loped swiftly across their path as if in frightened flight. As it disappeared, the reason became evident. An Indian boy about their own age came out of the woods. He stopped short upon seeing them.

He was dressed in clothes similar to theirs, but had coppery skin and straight black hair.

"Hello," he said pleasantly. "What are you fellows doing so deep in the woods? Lost?"

Neither Chet nor the Hardys answered at once. They were staring at the moccasins the boy was wearing. On each toe section was the mysterious R, outlined with multicoloured beads.

"No, we're not lost," Frank replied finally. "We're heading for the Ramapan village."

The Indian noticed the boys' eyes riveted on his moccasins. "What is it?" he asked with a puzzled air.

"Where did you get those moccasins?" Joe questioned him excitedly.

"Why, right here," replied the youth. "We Ramapans make them."

"You are a Ramapan?" Frank asked.

"Sure."

Joe seized the Indian's hand joyfully. "Are we glad to see you! We've been trying for days to find out who makes those moccasins!"

"Well, follow me, then," the boy said, smiling. "I can show you plenty more like these. By the way, I'm Ted Whitestone. My father is Chief Oscar Whitestone of the Ramapans."

The Hardys and Chet introduced themselves. Then Ted turned in the direction of his village.

"Quite a difference between Ted and that man we met on the trail," Joe whispered to his brother as Chet asked Ted questions about his tribe.

"No, we don't live in teepees," the Indian boy replied with a smile. "Just regular houses like everybody else. And we don't dress up in feathers and big war bonnets, either. I hope I'm not disillusioning you fellows," he added with a grin.

"But we heard tom-toms," said Chet.

"One of the men was practising for our ceremonial dance that we always perform at this time of year," Ted explained.

"And we saw an Indian dressed in fringed leather just a few minutes before we met you," Chet told him. "He had a peculiar accent."

Ted's eyes widened in surprise. "That's funny. I can't imagine who it might be. Nobody in our tribe dresses like that or talks with an accent, except old Long Heart, and he's all right. What did the man want?"

Frank told him of the stranger's warning about the Ramapans and how they would resent the boys' presence because the tribe was guarding a secret.

"That's crazy," Ted declared. "I can't understand

why a stranger would want to keep you from coming here. I'll speak to my father about this."

The young detectives glanced at one another. Were they bringing trouble to the Ramapans, or were they running into some?

"Here we are," Ted announced as the path suddenly widened and opened into a spacious cleared area.

The Ramapan village consisted of a main street with stores and several side roads with small, neat houses, most of them painted white. Off to one side stood a long, low building with many windows in it, and in the other direction was a large field which Ted said was used for athletics and tribal conferences.

"This is my home," Ted said, stopping before a small white house with green shutters.

A tall, distinguished-looking man, whom the youth resembled, met them at the door.

"Dad," Ted addressed him, "I'd like you to meet Frank and Joe Hardy and Chet Morton."

The boys and Chief Oscar Whitestone shook hands, then smiling warmly, the man added, "Come in, boys. You've had a long hike. We don't often see strangers this deep in the forest."

When Frank told him briefly why they had come, Chief Whitestone was greatly interested.

"We'll show you the factory where we make our leather products," he said.

The boys followed Chief Whitestone and his son outside. As the group walked towards the factory, the villagers gave cheery greetings to the head of their tribe. Reaching the long, low building which the boys had noticed before, the chief led the way inside.

"Here's where we do our handicraft work," Ted spoke up proudly, his arm encompassing the long room with a single broad sweep.

As they walked down one of the aisles, Ted's father explained the various kinds of work the craftsmen were doing. "This man is making moccasins," he said.

The visitors peered over the shoulder of an old Indian who was carefully moulding strips of leather over a wooden block. They could see the outlines of the footwear taking shape.

"Those workers over there are sewing key cases," Chief Whitestone pointed out. The boys watched as one of them punched a hole in the leather with an awl and expertly drew the thread through.

Frank produced the key case their mother had brought from Breck. "Ever seen this before?" he asked Chief Whitestone.

The Indian examined the leather article carefully. "Certainly. It was made right here," he answered. He was about to hand it back when he took another look inside. "Just as I thought, Ted. This is made of that special leather we had. It was in that suitcase full of our work that was stolen a few weeks ago." Turning to Frank, he added, "Where did you come across this?"

The boy explained that they were amateur detectives and related the events of the past few days concerning Breck, who had sold the key case to Mrs Hardy, Kamp his lawyer, and the man in the blue sweater who had tried to gain access to Mr Hardy's secret filing cabinet.

"I suppose you have no idea who took the suitcase,

Chief Whitestone," Joe said, unable to hide his disappointment.

"I'm afraid I haven't," the chief replied. "You see," he explained, "all our work is carried out of here in suitcases, since we can't get a truck or car through the trail. Then it's taken by train to Williamsville, where it's turned over to a distributor. He markets everything for us."

The boys listened carefully as the chief went on, "A couple of weeks ago our messenger left a suitcase unguarded in the railway station, and when he came back to get the bag, it was gone. That's all we know about it."

"I'd say we ought to leave here at once and track down Breck," said Frank, "if it weren't for the strange man we met in the woods. He's probably connected with this mystery. I think we'll stay round Lantern Junction for a few days and try to find him."

"I wish you luck," Chief Whitestone said. When they were outside again, he turned to face Frank and Joe.

"So you're detectives," he remarked. "And you're staying round here for a while."

"That's right," Frank replied, wondering what the chief was leading up to.

Smiling at them, he asked, "How would you like to solve a mystery for me—an old mystery of the Ramapans?"

·11·

A Jewelled Dagger

ANOTHER mystery to solve!

"We'll do our best, Chief Whitestone," Frank said.

"And when he tells you that," Chet spoke up, "it means they'll solve it."

Ted and his father smiled as the young detectives blushed at the compliment.

"When can we start?" Joe asked. "We'd like to begin right now because we're due back at school in a week or so."

"Yes, and it depends a little on where we'll have to go," Frank added. "Is it far away?"

"You can begin right here and now," the chief replied. "In fact, you'll have to solve the mystery in the next few days or else wait a whole year."

With this baffling introduction he invited the boys to go back to his home and hear the full story. Seated before an open fire in a cosy room filled with Indian relics, he began the strange tale.

"We Ramapans are an old tribe. We were once a great and powerful nation, a leader among the Indians in this part of the country.

"But as the years passed, and the white men spread out, our territories grew smaller. Our people became fewer in number as tribal warfare and sickness took their toll. Gradually the Ramapans' power was so weakened that we were forced to move north. This was many generations ago.

"Then, finally, the wars stopped, and modern medicine cut down our death rate. We became prosperous, but still we were small and missed our former greatness," he said with a faraway look.

"The tribe carefully held on to its savings from fishing and trapping. Then fifty-nine years ago the leaders made a decision. With my father as chief, they decided to pool their resources and move down from the wild north country. The place they chose was this very acreage, the site where our ancestors had lived."

The boys had scarcely moved as the fascinating tale unfolded.

"My father and the tribe bought this land from the estate of a man named York."

York! The name of one of the suspected gang!

"Was his name Philip York?" Frank asked.

"No," Chief Whitestone replied. "It was Amos York. But after the tribe set up their new home, they didn't find the peace and security they had expected."

"What happened?" Joe asked.

The chief had paused to strike a match to his long pipe. He puffed a few times, then continued. "A neighbouring tribe started to raid the Ramapans. They came every night, stealing and destroying our property and striking terror in the hearts of our people. But the Ramapans fought back even against heavy odds.

"My father was fearful the enemy would steal our deed to the property, as well as other valuable tribal records. So he buried them secretly, together with a jewelled dagger worth thousands of dollars that the Ramapans had had in their possession for generations. They had confiscated it after a battle with a French army two hundred years previously."

"Where did your father bury the papers and the dagger?" Frank asked him.

Chief Whitestone shook his head. "That's the mystery. Shortly afterwards, he became ill and finally we realized he was dying.

"According to the laws of our tribe, I would become chief. Everyone knew my father had buried the papers and the dagger, but the place was a secret. So I asked him where they were.

"He was sinking rapidly, but he opened his eyes with great will power and whispered: 'My son—my son—papers—dagger—buried where a crisscross shadow is cast in the light of the hunter's moon."

As the chief stopped speaking, there was complete silence for several seconds, then the Hardys looked at Chet. His face wore a smug look, as if to say: "There *is* a treasure buried in a crisscross shadow!"

Chief Whitestone continued after a moment. "That was the only clue my father gave and I've never been able to find the place."

"It doesn't sound like an easy task," Frank remarked. "We—"

"That's not all," Chief Whitestone interrupted. "Not long ago two strangers appeared in the village. They said they wished to buy our land and were prepared to offer a fair price.

" 'No,' I told them, 'we wouldn't sell for all the

money in the world. This is our home. The tribe has grown and prospered here after many generations of hardship. Our land is not for sale.' "

"But that didn't end it," Ted took up the story. "The men were insistent. Finally, one of them became angry and started to yell. 'Look, Chief,' he said to my father, 'I'm warning you! You'd better sell to us if you know what's good for you.' "

"That's right." Chief Whitestone nodded. " 'What do you mean?' I asked them.

" 'Just this,' the man replied. 'This land isn't yours.'

"I laughed at that, but he said, 'You think it's funny, eh? Well, we can prove you haven't got a clear title!' Then they stamped out of the house and disappeared.

"I'm afraid those men will find the deed before we do and steal it," Chief Whitestone said. "Unfortunately we have no other proof of ownership. The courthouse, where our deed was recorded, was burned down a few years ago and the papers were lost."

"Then those men can make it very hard for you," Joe said.

"Yes. After the fire, advertisements were run in the papers for people to bring in their deeds and have them recorded again, but we couldn't do that, of course."

"So it was easy for those men to find out your deed is missing," Frank surmised. "Well, we'll certainly try to find it for you."

"Haven't you any protection?" Chet interposed.

"Yes," the chief said. "After sixty years of possession, the tribe will own the land automatically—even without a deed. It's a state law. But we have several months to go before the time is up. Until then, we're at the mercy of anyone who finds those papers! And we can't be certain someone hasn't already taken them, of course."

"I doubt it," Frank commented. "If they had, either the papers would have been returned by honest people, or you would have had trouble before this with real thieves."

"How about those men who were here?" Chief Whitestone asked.

"I don't think they would have offered to buy the land if they could have had it free."

"But I'll bet they're looking for the deed," Joe remarked. "So it's going to be a race. Let's get started!"

"I like your enthusiasm." The chief smiled. "But first I suggest we have something to eat. And later, why don't you move in here so that you can be handy to your work?"

"Thank you," Frank replied. "We'll do that. Along with solving your mystery, we'll do some sleuthing on our own case."

By the time they had finished a meal of venison, corn bread, and fried apples prepared by Mrs Whitestone, it had grown dark.

"You'd better make do tonight," Ted suggested. "You can go back and get your things at the hotel tomorrow."

The boys accepted Ted's hospitality and slept on camp beds in his room.

After breakfast the next morning, Joe said, "First thing we'll have to do is move our belongings in from town."

"Right you are," Frank agreed. "But there's no need

for all of us to go back. I'll go and put all we need in one bag and check the others in at the left luggage."

"Then Chet and I will start hunting round here for clues," Joe declared.

Chet went to question some of the older men of the tribe. Joe ambled along the street until he reached the leathercraft building. Nonchalantly he walked round the outside of it to observe the layout of the structure.

"Guess I'll go inside," Joe told himself. "Maybe if I talk to some of the workers—"

The sound of a door opening interrupted his thoughts. He stood motionless as he saw one of the craftsmen emerge from the rear entrance. Joe ducked behind a tree and watched as the man looked intently in every direction.

"He acts as though he doesn't want to be seen," Joe thought.

Abruptly the man turned and set out briskly through the forest. Joe trailed him noiselessly.

Suddenly the Indian stopped and Joe concealed himself behind an evergreen. The man began stripping bark from a tree, all the while whistling in a carefree manner.

Joe, puzzled, rose slowly from his hiding place. "If that's all that guy came here for," he mused, "why did he act as though he were scared of being seen?"

The next moment the Indian lit a cigarette. After a few puffs he stamped it out and started back for the crafts building.

Joe grinned as he recalled a *No Smoking* sign in the building.

"So he just slipped out to have a smoke. He sure had me fooled."

Joe started walking back towards the village. Suddenly he stopped in his tracks. What was that strange scraping noise behind him off to the right?

He stealthily retraced his steps in the direction of the sound, which led him to a small clearing. Joe barely restrained an exclamation when he saw a man digging in the hard-packed earth.

It was the stranger in the suède-fringed suit whom the boys had met the day before!

Without hesitation, Joe approached the digger.

"Now I'll find out what his game is," he was thinking when a twig snapped behind him.

Joe looked over his shoulder in time to see a man leaping towards him, brandishing a stick.

He tried to duck, but the man brought the stick smashing down on the boy's head.

Without uttering a cry, Joe crumpled to the earth!

A Puzzling Telegram

A QUARTER of an hour passed before Joe stirred. Opening his eyes, he was conscious only of a severe pain in the top of his head. Feeling the damp earth against his cheek, the young detective realized he was lying on the ground.

With what seemed like a superhuman effort, Joe lifted himself on one elbow and saw the trees about him. Only then did he remember what had occurred. He put his hand to his head and felt a large bump.

"I'd better get back to the Ramapan village," he muttered. "Got to warn Chief Whitestone about those men."

His head throbbed. Swaying from side to side, Joe took a few uncertain steps. It was hard going but finally he reached the edge of the village. There he saw a familiar figure hurrying up the street.

"Chet!" He tried to shout, but his words were barely audible and his friend turned a corner out of sight. Joe started for the Whitestone house, stopping frequently to rest.

Suddenly he heard a cry behind him. "Joe! What happened?"

"Ted! Oh, gosh, I'm glad to see you."

"Who hit you?" Ted exclaimed, seeing a huge, bloody lump on the top of Joe's head.

"Don't know," he gasped as the Indian boy steered him towards his house.

As they reached the steps, Chief Whitestone came out. He helped Ted lift Joe and soon the injured youth was resting on a couch.

Ted hurried for the village doctor. After a thorough examination the physician concluded that there was no skull fracture, but told Joe that he might have a headache for a few hours and to call him if anything else developed. He dressed the wound and left.

A sigh escaped Ted's lips. "Thought you were a goner when I saw you staggering down that street, Joe," he said, and smiled in relief.

But Chief Whitestone was not smiling.

"That fellow tried to kill you!" he exclaimed. He clenched his pipe, the knuckles showing white against the dark bowl.

"Ted," he went on, "I'm very much concerned about this business. I want you to make inquiries round the village while Joe takes it easy."

"Don't worry about me, Chief Whitestone," Joe insisted. "We detectives are used to some roughing up now and then."

"Did you get a good look at the man who hit you?" Ted wanted to know.

"Yes. But I've never seen him before. I couldn't identify him," Joe said ruefully.

At that moment Chet hurried in, having heard from a child that the doctor had been calling on "the sick white boy."

"Joe!" he exclaimed, pale with fright. "What happened?"

While Chet was listening to Joe's story, Frank Hardy strode briskly down the forest trail and finally reached Lantern Junction. He went at once to the Grand Hotel.

"We're moving out," he told the pleasant clerk.

"Going home so soon?"

"No. We're staying with the Ramapans. If any messages come here, we'll pay to have them delivered up there in care of the chief."

"Glad to oblige you," the clerk said.

After paying the bill, packing, and arranging for all the bags but one to be left at the hotel, Frank decided to telephone his mother.

She herself answered. "Frank? What a relief to hear from you!"

"Anything wrong?" he wanted to know, detecting a note of agitation in Mrs Hardy's voice.

"Yes. I was afraid those men might have been after you and Joe again. There's been another attempted burglary of our house!"

Frank grabbed at the mouthpiece. "Are you and Aunt Gertrude all right? Did you see the burglar? Did he get anything?"

"We're all right," Mrs Hardy replied quickly. "But the burglar got away. I can't tell you whether he stole anything or not. Chief Collig is working on the case right now.

"There's more news of your father," his mother went on.

"Is it good news?"

"Well, I don't know. Another case of sabotage," Mrs Hardy told him. "This time in St Louis. A laboratory was swept by flames last night and the reports of secret experiments went up in smoke. Dad was reported on the scene."

"Good!" Frank exclaimed. "At least the investigations in capable hands."

"But I'm worried, son. I tried to get in touch with your father in St Louis through the police, but the authorities there told me he had disappeared."

"Disappeared!" Frank repeated anxiously, then said, "Maybe he's only gone underground to track down the gang."

"I don't know what to think, Frank," Mrs Hardy replied. "Just a little while ago I got a message that has me completely baffled."

"Message from Dad?"

"Yes. And it came from California! All the telegram said was '*Detained in California. Will wire again.*' "

"But the report of the sabotage placed Dad in St Louis."

"Exactly." Mrs Hardy sighed. "I think the wire from California is a hoax!"

"Something's fishy, that's sure," Frank agreed. "But don't worry. I have an idea. I'll let you know when I learn something.

"All right, dear, and give my love to Joe."

Frank clicked the phone, then asked the operator to connect him with John Bryant in San Francisco. The man was a detective friend of Fenton Hardy and could be depended upon.

"Hello, Frank. Glad to hear from you. Great things your father's doing these days."

"That's why I'm calling. We're worried about reports that he's in two places at once."

Mr Bryant chuckled. "I didn't think even a Hardy could do that."

Frank quickly explained the mystery of his father's seemingly double appearances.

"This is my plan," he said, speaking guardedly. "Will you check on Dad at his hotel, and then wire the result to Sam Radley at the Bayport Hospital? It's important that you send the message to Sam. One to us would probably be intercepted or tampered with. Mother's been getting some, but she thinks they may be phonies."

Assuring Frank of his fullest co-operation, Mr Bryant said good-bye.

"I'd better warn Sam Radley to expect a message from Mr Bryant," Frank thought, and hurried to a writing desk.

After penning a few lines to his father's injured operative, Frank folded the paper and inserted it in an envelope which he addressed in plain block letters to disguise his handwriting. He sealed the envelope, stamped it, and deposited the letter in a mailbox at the end of the lobby.

"Nobody will dare tamper with Uncle Sam's mail," he told himself in satisfaction.

Waving to the desk clerk, Frank walked out of the hotel with his suitcase. As he turned down the street that led to the Ramapan trail, he saw a familiar figure hurrying towards him. It was Chet Morton!

Frank ran to meet Chet, who was gasping for breath from his exertions.

"Raced most of the way," he panted, "to tell you about—about Joe. Attacked by stranger—knocked out!" Chet heaved as he tried to regain his wind.

"Knocked out! By whom? Tell me!" Frank shook Chet in his excitement.

Sitting down on the kerb, and pausing frequently to get his breath, Chet recounted Joe's experience in the woods.

"The doctor's seen him. He'll be okay. I came to town for the police."

"Go on," Frank urged.

Chet rose, his breathing restored. "Ted and I went to find Joe's attacker," he said.

"Any luck?" Frank asked. He was seething at the thought of his brother being so brutally assaulted.

"We located the spot where the man attacked Joe," Chet replied, "and searched the area. Finally we saw tracks leading to the main trail and followed them for a few yards until they were lost."

"Did you find any other clue?" Frank asked, disappointed that they had not caught Joe's assailant.

Chet grinned in satisfaction. "We found this."

Digging inside his jacket, he produced a package wrapped in cloth.

"What is it?" Frank asked, puzzled.

Chet unwrapped the cloth. "A piece of the stick used on Joe!"

"Good work, Chet!" Frank cried.

Carefully he examined the piece. One end was splintered, showing that it had been broken by a violent blow.

"You're taking this to the police?" he asked.

"Sure. For fingerprints!"

The boys went at once. Frank gave the desk sergeant their names and asked for the Chief. The visitors were ushered into his office.

"Frank Hardy, eh?" he greeted them. He was a short, plump man, who gave the boys a warm smile and told them to call him Mike. "Any relation to Fenton Hardy, the famous detective?"

"His son. My brother's at the Ramapan village."

"Well, well," the officer said. "What brings you boys up to this neck of the woods? Some mystery?"

Quickly Frank explained their mission to find a thief named Breck. When he told the officer what had happened to Joe, the police chief looked grave.

"Any clues?" he asked.

Chet produced the stick and told about finding it near the spot where Joe had been attacked.

"I thought the fellow's fingerprints might be on it," he added hopefully.

"It won't take long to find out," Mike replied, then carried the piece of wood into a back room.

While he was gone, the boys talked over the various aspects of the mystery, and Frank whispered the latest news about his father.

"Good grief!" Chet exclaimed.

A short while later the officer returned, a satisfied look on his face. In one hand he carried a Manila folder.

"Well, Chet," he said, "you hit the jackpot. We found a jailbird's fingerprints on this stick!"

A broad grin broke over the boy's face. Frank congratulated him.

"Whose prints are they?" he asked.

Mike opened the folder and took out some papers. "Fellow by the name of Smirkis," he told them. "About forty years old. Small-time crook. Got a year for robbery some months back. He was released a short time ago for good behaviour. Lives right here in town."

"Smirkis, eh?" Frank mused. "I wonder if he's connected with the gang we're after."

"I couldn't say. He wasn't too bad a fellow, but he may have met someone in prison who put ideas in his head," Mike said.

"Where does he live?" Frank asked.

"We've just checked with his landlady, but she said he hasn't been home in a couple of days. I've sent out an alarm for him.

"We'll need your brother to identify Smirkis as the assailant when we catch up with him. Meanwhile, take care of yourselves," Mike warned.

The boys thanked him, ate a light lunch, and then headed back to the Indian village. Frank was anxious to see Joe and was glad to find him feeling better.

Next day, while Joe was recuperating, he discussed the clue to the missing papers and the jewelled dagger with Frank, Chet, and Ted. Chief Whitestone had gone to Lantern Junction on business.

" 'Buried where a crisscross shadow is cast in the light of the hunter's moon,' " Chet mulled over the chief's statement. "Wonder what made the crisscross shadow."

He and Joe made several suggestions that were immediately discounted by Ted because they did not agree with the legend.

"The story goes this way. 'And the chief buried the dagger of the many bright eyes and the papers of the paleface writing while at his hunter's dwelling in the early moonrise.' "

"Hunter's dwelling!" Frank cried. "I have it!"

·13·

The Hunter's Moon

"WHAT?" Joe, Chet, and Ted chorused in surprise.

"A hunter's dwelling," Frank explained, "could be a teepee. The crisscross shadow was made by the poles!"

"Of course!" Ted exclaimed. "Why didn't we Ramapans think of that?"

"And the hunter's moon is in October, isn't it?" Chet asked.

"Yes, it's the full moon of October and it rises early just like the legend says," Ted answered. "In October the angle the moon makes with the earth is very slight, so it rises as the full moon very soon after sunset."

"We're going into the hunter's moon right now," Frank said. "That's what your father meant, Ted, when he urged us to solve the mystery soon!"

"Yes."

"First thing to do," Frank went on, "is to find out where the chief's teepee stood when he buried the treasure. Have you any idea where that was?" he asked Ted.

"It was near where the tribe used to hold its ceremonials," Ted replied. "The records say that the ceremonial rock was located where a stream, forked like a serpent's tongue, cuts through the warrior's place of honour."

"What does that mean?" Chet questioned.

"Long ago, returning warriors were honoured for a whole day by feasting and—"

"Sounds good." The stout boy beamed. "They probably had roast moose and—"

"Let's get going," Frank interrupted.

Ted led the way to the area where the old ceremonials had been held. He said that it had not been used in his lifetime.

"Then we're going to have a hard job locating the rock in this overgrown tangle," Joe remarked, looking about him.

He had insisted upon going along but the others made him sit on the side lines and not exert himself. Disgusted, Joe sat down on a log which had fallen across what once had been the fork in the stream mentioned in the legend.

"Looks as if we're stumped," he said ten minutes later when the boys found no evidence of a large flat rock.

Frank, who had squatted down near him and was staring in the direction of the main stream, suddenly gave a shout.

"There it is, fellows!"

He ran towards a little mound of silt and moss that they had overlooked in their search. Digging excitedly for a few seconds, and scraping away the encrustation of many years, he exposed a huge, flat rock to the light.

"And now to find out where the chief's teepee stood," Joe said.

"It's beyond me," Chet commented, and wearily sat down on the rock.

"Paleface boy want to know where old chief's teepee stood?" a voice behind him said.

Chet jumped in surprise and whirled round to look at an elderly Indian wearing a leather shirt and leggings.

"Hello, Long Heart," Ted greeted the old man.

The boys had seen him around the village, dressed in the outmoded costume of the Ramapans. Ted introduced him as the oldest member of the tribe.

"He's always telling us stories of the old days," Ted said, smiling.

"We do want to know where the old chief's teepee stood," Frank said. "Can you help us?"

"My memory not so good—for I am many moons old," Long Heart answered. "But maybe remember where teepee of great brave stood."

With that, he started walking back and forth, muttering to himself. Finally he stopped two hundred feet from the ceremonial rock.

"Here," he said with finality. "Here teepee of chief. Why paleface want know this?" he asked Ted suspiciously.

After the boy told him the palefaces were trying to find the lost deed in order to save the tribe's land, the old brave's eyes lighted up.

"Me help," he said simply. "You build teepee with pole fifteen feet long. Me come tonight at rise of moon." Saying no more, he turned his back and went towards the village.

"How do you build a Ramapan teepee?" Chet asked. "Is it any different from the ones we made at camp?"

"Probably not." Ted grinned. "I guess you palefaces learned how from us Indians."

Nevertheless, he instructed them as they began their work. They cut down six saplings fifteen feet long and tied them together three feet from the top. Then they raised the poles and spread the legs to form a firm base, pressing them into the ground.

The next step was to lash short, flexible saplings horizontally across the slanting poles. After that, they fastened sections of birch and hemlock bark over them with tough vines and trailing roots. Short poles were used to cover the bark to keep it from curling.

Finally they cut a smoke hole at the top and another for an entrance. The boys stood back proudly to view their work.

"Pretty swell," Chet remarked. "Now if that old moon'll just come out, we'll find that deed for your dad in no time, Ted," he boasted.

"I suppose it's expecting too much to keep this operation a secret from our enemies," Frank remarked. "But let's come here separately tonight and watch for any spies."

"Agreed," they all said.

Just before sunset the Hardys, Chet, Ted, and Chief Whitestone, going by separate routes, arrived at the old ceremonial rock. They found Long Heart waiting impassively for them.

"The weather's holding up," Frank said to Joe.

Slowly the sun sank below the horizon. Then a few minutes later the hunter's moon of the legend shone from behind some clouds. Eagerly six pairs of eyes followed the clouds until they blew away.

Suddenly Joe whispered excitedly, "There it is—the crisscross shadow!"

It was true. The poles atop the teepee made crisscrossed shadows on the moonlit ground.

"Let's dig!" Ted cried, grasping one of the shovels they had brought along.

With grim determination the group sank their spades into the earth and started working.

Would they uncover the missing papers and the jewelled dagger? each one wondered, the silent chief most of all.

The mound of earth beside the hole swiftly grew higher as the pit widened and deepened under the eager labours of the treasure hunters.

Finally Frank paused and leaned on his shovel. "Whew!" he said. "It may be cold by the thermometer, but I'm sure hot."

"Me too," Chet puffed. "This digging is getting harder the farther down we go." He stood in a wide hole up to his knees.

"It's very rocky in this country," Chief Whitestone remarked.

After a rest, the four plunged their spades into the hard-packed earth with renewed vigour. The bright hunter's moon cast an eerie light over the scene, with stalwart Long Heart standing guard.

Joe, regretting that he was not in condition to help the others, stationed himself in the shadow of the teepee, keeping alert for any intruder—accidental or planned.

Suddenly he tensed. He strained his ears to catch a sound over the hard breathing of his friends and the soft thuds the earth made as it was shovelled from the pit. The sound came again.

"A twig being stepped on in the woods," Joe told himself. "I'd better have a look!"

Quietly he slipped among the trees from which the mysterious crackling had come. Joe peered through the maze of moonlight and shadows. Ahead he thought he could detect a man moving silently among the trees!

He tried to follow the ghostly figure. But it kept eluding him and finally disappeared. Wondering who it could have been, Joe retraced his steps to the clearing where the others were still working.

"Find anything yet?" Joe called out.

Chief Whitestone tossed his shovel aside and clambered out of the hole. The others followed.

"Not a thing!" he replied to Joe.

"We're getting no place here," Frank said. "I guess it's useless to dig any more. There are certainly no buried papers in this spot."

"Looks as if you're right," Ted agreed. "I guess we had the wrong spot for the teepee, or the wrong crisscross shadow."

In the moonlight the disappointment on everyone's face was easily seen.

"Buck up, fellows," Joe said encouragingly. "Maybe after a good night's sleep we can figure out where we failed to interpret the clue in the legend correctly."

"Right you are, Joe," the chief said. "Let's return home. We'll all have hot drinks, then go straight to bed."

As the others gathered up their tools, Joe took Frank aside. Swiftly he told him of the incident in the woods, and his suspicions that the group had been spied upon by a prowler.

"No use worrying the others about it," he said. "Listen! Let's stay overnight in the teepee and keep watch for intruders."

"Great idea," Frank agreed. "The teepee's weather-tight, and we'll bring some blankets."

Chief Whitestone and Ted protested strongly when they heard of the plan, but the Hardys insisted.

As the others trooped slowly out of the clearing back to the village, Frank glanced at the moon. "Look!" he pointed. "Clouds up there. Bad weather ahead."

"Let's hurry and get things ready for the night," Joe suggested. "We'll need a fire."

Quickly they gathered dead pine limbs and brush and in a short while had a small, cheerful fire blazing inside the teepee. Chet returned with several blankets, then said good night.

As the boys finished adjusting the bark door, Joe held out his hand. "Snow," he said. "Well, I'll take the first watch. You get some sleep."

In a few moments Frank's regular breathing indicated he was asleep. Wrapping up warmly, Joe took up his guard duty. The early snow began falling more thickly. After a couple of hours, he wakened his brother.

"How's the weather?" Frank asked.

"Snowing pretty hard. Nothing stirring out there. But keep your eyes open," he warned.

During Frank's watch the snow gradually turned to fine rain, but by the time he changed watches, it had stopped.

"Starting to turn mighty cold out there," he said as Joe took up his post.

Morning finally came. The temperature was down a good bit, and when the dawn broke, the clearing and the woods were covered with a dazzling glaze of ice.

There was a rustling at the bark door to the teepee and Ted poked his head through the opening.

"Good morning, fellows. Anything happen during the night?"

"Not a thing," Frank replied.

But Joe was staring intently at a man who was emerging stealthily from the underbrush. As the stranger reached the clearing, Joe cried out in startled recognition:

"That's my attacker!"

With a leap, he charged the mysterious fellow and tripped him.

"Good going!" Frank cried.

In a moment Ted pinned his hands behind his back, and the man was their prisoner.

"You're the guy who whacked me—Smirkis!" Joe said accusingly.

"All right, I'm Smirkis. But I never whacked any of you," the man protested.

"No? Well, your fingerprints were on the stick. What's more, I saw you sneaking round while we were digging last night!"

"No, I didn't spy on you." Smirkis shook his head vigorously, but he had paled at Joe's mention of the fingerprints.

"You'd better come with us to police headquarters," Frank said.

"Wait a minute!" Smirkis cried out anxiously. "I'll make a deal with you."

"What kind of deal?" Joe asked.

"If you'll let me go, I'll give you some vital information. How about it?" he whined.

The boys looked at one another questioningly. It was attractive bait that Smirkis was offering. His vital information might lead to the solution of the mystery!

Joe and Frank moved out of the man's hearing to talk it over. "I don't trust him," Joe whispered.

Frank nodded. "Let's try to trick him."

He turned to Smirkis. "I know what you're going to tell us. That the men who want to buy this property hired you to get rid of us!"

"How'd you know that?" Smirkis gasped.

No sooner had he uttered the words than a strange voice behind them cried, "Shut up!"

Frank and Joe wheeled round to face three masked men, poised to attack!

·14·

A Rough Trip

As the Hardys leaped at their attackers, one of the masked men side-stepped them to clamp a hand over Ted's mouth as he started to give the Ramapan war cry for help. Locked in a fierce struggle, Joe and Frank hurled their opponents to the ground. The boys fought with every bit of strength they could muster, but the odds were against them.

"Okay, tie 'em up and blindfold 'em," ordered one of the men, who seemed to be the leader.

The arms of the young detectives and their Indian friend were tightly bound and their eyes covered with kerchiefs.

"All set?" the same voice asked. "Let's go! You know the plan, men."

Frank and Joe were roughly grasped by the shoulders and pushed.

"Start walking," the leader ordered.

As they trudged off, the Hardys heard sounds heading in another direction.

"They're separating us from Ted," Joe whispered to Frank.

"Keep quiet!" the leader commanded.

"You won't be so anxious to stick your noses in

other people's business when we get through with you," one of the men sneered.

"You can't win, anyway," the leader said. "In a short while the Indians will be gone!"

"You're trying to bluff us," Frank spoke up boldly.

"Bluffing, you say? Just wait and see. This land's going to change hands, and you can't stop it!"

After a long silence, one of the men said, "What about Smirkis? He talks too much!"

"The boss'll take care of him after he does that job for us."

So Smirkis was the one who had taken Ted away!

Presently the boys were halted. Then hands lifted them up and lowered them into a canoe.

"Okay," the leader said. "Let's shove off."

After a silent trip of an hour or so the bottom of the canoe scraped against sand, and in a moment the boys were jerked to their feet and dragged across the ground. Next they were lifted into a vehicle with its engine running. They started off over a rough road.

Joe and Frank were ravenous, not having eaten for many hours, but the men made no offer of food. The car rumbled on for what seemed an eternity.

"We must be a long way from the Ramapans by now!" Frank thought. "Where are we going?"

Almost an hour later the car stopped. The prisoners were hauled out. The wind was blowing in gusts as if a storm were brewing.

"What next?" the Hardys thought, then heard a plane's motor being tuned up. They were hoisted into the craft and it took off.

Judging by the way they were being jolted up and

down, Frank and Joe realized that they had been stowed in the tail section.

It was a rough trip, with no chance for them to try to loosen their bonds. The plane rose and fell with dizzying speed as it was buffeted by the wind. The drumming of hail indicated that the storm was becoming more violent, and the swift changes of pressure on their eardrums were painful.

When the plane finally landed, the prisoners were gagged. Then they were carried out, thrown into a car, and driven a distance. After a while the car halted and the boys were pushed up a flight of stairs.

"Okay," the leader ordered curtly, "cover your own faces and then take off their blindfolds."

The Hardys blinked as the light, though dim, struck their eyes. Peering round, they found themselves in a gloomy, shabbily furnished room. Their masked captors surrounded them menacingly.

Suddenly the young detectives caught sight of a transparent curtain near one end of the room. A figure was seated behind it, half turned towards them.

The boys gasped. "Dad!" they cried out, shocked by what they saw. Mr Hardy looked badly mauled and mistreated. His clothes were creased and dirt-streaked. His head hung in an attitude of complete defeat!

The masked leader addressed the boys. "You've been wondering about your father. Now you know. Mr Hardy, your sons are here. Speak to them."

"Boys," he said, without moving, "you can't beat these men. Give up!"

Astonished, Frank and Joe tried to break loose and rush to him. But quickly the strong hands of their captors reached out and halted them. They were whisked into an adjoining room and flung violently on to the floor.

Their blindfolds were replaced and tape was fastened over their lips in place of the gags.

"That ought to hold you," the leader snarled as they struggled in vain, "until you go on your next trip."

The boys wondered what he meant, but an explanation was immediately forthcoming.

"We'll be back to put you on a freighter," he went on, "and when it reaches its destination, you won't be in a position to bother anybody!"

The door slammed and footfalls told the Hardys that the men had gone. After waiting to make sure that a guard had not been posted, they struggled with their bonds, grunting and panting behind their sealed lips. But their captors had done their work well. The ropes would not budge an inch! Exhausted, they sprawled on the door.

Suddenly Frank got an idea. "It might work," he told himself hopefully.

Crawling over to Joe, he raised himself erect, using his brother's body as a prop. Slipping his bound wrists over the doorknob, he wriggled his hands round and round.

Finally one of the bonds loosened, then another. Frank twisted his hands violently. The ropes slipped. he was free!

Quickly he ripped off the blindfold and the adhesive tape, then released his brother.

"Thank goodness!" Joe whispered. "Now to break out of here!"

Rubbing their chafed wrists, the boys surveyed the dingy little room. The only exit was the door. When it refused to open, Joe said:

"Come on. Let's crash it!"

Rearing back, they heaved against the door. Once, twice, then a loud splintering noise and the door gave way.

Crashing into the other room, they looked for their father. But he as well as the men had vanished!

"They've taken Dad with them!" Joe cried.

"Come on," Frank urged. "Let's get out of here. We have work to do to save him!"

The boys dashed down the stairs and into the street. They gazed round them.

"This place looks familiar," Frank said, then added excitedly as he saw a store sign, "we're in Southport!"

"Let's get to the police fast, Frank," Joe urged, "before those men get too far away with Dad!"

"Hold on a minute!" Frank exclaimed, a strange look coming over his face. "There's something mighty queer about this whole deal. Before we see the police, I suggest that we get in touch with Mother and with Sam Radley."

"You suspect something?" Joe asked.

"I sure do!"

·15·

The Hideout

"THAT wasn't Dad at all," Frank told Joe.

"What!"

"Bet you anything! He'd have given us some sign."

"But it was his voice," Joe protested.

"That's the only part which puzzles me," Frank confessed. "Before we go to the police, let's check with Sam Radley and find out whether he's heard from Mr Bryant."

"Good idea. But how about some food?"

"You find a taxi and I'll grab some sandwiches."

"With what?" Joe asked.

Frank realized ruefully that they did not have any money and knew no one in town but the police.

"I guess we'll have to go to them after all and borrow some money."

They walked to headquarters and told their story. The captain said he would investigate the place at once. By the time the boys had washed, combed their hair, and brushed their clothes, the officers had returned. They reported that they could find no trace of the kidnappers.

"I'm sure they won't return," the captain commented, adding that Breck and York had not been seen in Southport.

The boys asked for a loan of ten dollars, then left. Munching sandwiches and drinking soda on their way in the taxi, they soon reached the Bayport Hospital.

Sam Radley was lying in bed reading. He looked up over the top of the paper.

"Why, hello, Frank and Joe. Where'd you come from?" the detective asked in astonishment.

"It's a long story," Frank replied. He briefly outlined their adventures, ending with his suspicion that the man at Southport was not Mr Hardy.

"You could be right," Sam conceded. "Here's a telegram from Mr Bryant." The message read:

STOP WORRYING ABOUT YOUR BOSS.

"That practically proves the man in Southport wasn't Dad," Frank said.

"Not necessarily," Sam replied. "It's just possible your father allowed himself to be captured on purpose to get closer to the gang and its operations."

"But why did he warn us to lay off?" Joe asked.

"For two reasons: so you wouldn't get hurt, and also so you wouldn't interfere with his sleuthing."

"That might be, but I still don't believe the man we saw in Southport was Dad."

"I don't agree with you, Frank," his brother declared. "I'm sure even an actor couldn't imitate Dad's voice so perfectly."

A gong sounded, and a nurse appeared. "Visitors must leave now," she said, and to be sure they did, she waited until the boys bade Sam good night and hurried down the corridor.

When they reached their home, Joe suddenly

grinned. "Mother and Aunt Gertrude will certainly be surprised to see us. They think that we're still up in the mountains."

"Who's there?" a suspicious voice called from behind the door.

"It's us, Aunt Gertrude," Frank answered.

The door swung open wide. "Joe! Frank!" she cried. "I'm glad you're home!"

"Who's there?" Mrs Hardy asked, coming to the hallway. "My boys!" she exclaimed, hugging them.

The reason for their sudden appearance was soon told. The women's eyes widened in amazement, and they asked them not to return to the dangerous area.

"But we don't know what happened to Ted White-stone!" Joe said. "He may be a prisoner."

"I understand," Mrs Hardy replied. "How about telephoning his father?"

"We'll do that, anyway," Frank said. "But if we're going to solve the Ramapan mystery, we must work before the hunter's moon is gone."

When he talked to Chief Whitestone, the man said a search had already been started for all three boys. He was amazed to hear what had happened, and was glad that the Hardys had escaped. The chief said grimly he would notify the police about Smirkis and the other men and that efforts to find his son would be re-doubled.

"We'll be back as soon as we can," Frank promised.

"That's fine, but I'm afraid Ted is miles away by this time," his father said woefully.

Joe phoned the airport and learned that a plane which left Bayport early in the morning stopped at

Lantern Junction. He quickly made reservations.

Meanwhile, Frank had begun to worry about the safety of his mother and Aunt Gertrude. He was afraid that when the gang found out the boys had escaped they might come to the Hardy home and seek revenge.

"I'm going to ask Chief Collig to post plainclothesmen at the house day and night," he said, and dialled the police headquarters.

Collig was not there, but he left the message with the sergeant who promised co-operation.

"A man will be here in a few minutes," Frank reported to his family.

He and Joe set an alarm clock and tumbled into bed. The next morning they found it hard to waken when the buzzer sounded, but they got up and dressed quickly. After kissing their aunt and mother good-bye, the boys left the house. They stopped for a moment to talk with the detective on guard, then started for the airport.

Arriving just in time, the Hardys took their seats in the small plane that serviced the mountainous region of the Ramapan country. An hour later they landed near Lantern Junction and were driven to town. After a hearty breakfast at the Grand Hotel they set out once more for the Indian village.

"We'd better keep our eyes open for anybody lying in wait for us," Frank advised. "I'll lead off and look in front and to the right. You check what's on our left and at the back of us."

But they saw no one and reached the Ramapan village without incident. When Chief Whitestone opened the door he grasped their hands eagerly.

"You're back! But there's no word of Ted! You have no idea where he might be?"

"I'm afraid, Chief Whitestone," Frank said, "that he's a prisoner of the people who are trying to get your land away from you."

The Indian stared unbelievingly. "You mean they're holding him as a hostage?"

"Probably."

"I had no idea what danger you'd get into when I asked you to find the deed," the chief said. "We've looked in vain for Ted so far. Chet and some of the villagers as well as the police are out now hunting for him. Have you anything to suggest?"

The boys said they were so sure that Smirkis was holding Ted prisoner, that they would base their efforts on that assumption.

"Let's phone Mike right away," said Frank.

He dashed to the telephone. Seconds later he realized that the line was dead.

"More of the gang's work," Frank said in disgust. "They've cut the line!"

Joe suggested that he and Frank hurry to town and tell their story to the police. Without waiting for Chet, they returned to Lantern Junction and went to headquarters.

"We think Ted was taken away by Smirkis," Joe said. "Can you tell us anything about his haunts so that we can look for him too?"

Mike ran his fingers through his hair before replying. Suddenly he snapped his fingers.

"The cabin!" he exclaimed. "That's the place. It just came to me. Smirkis once had a hunting cabin in the woods. He sold it, but I'll bet that's where he's hiding."

The Hardys were on their feet in an instant. "Come on!" said Frank. "Let's have a look right away!"

The officer got his car and they drove a couple of miles out of town. Mike parked and they started off through a heavily overgrown area.

After a twenty-minute trek Mike suddenly held up his hand and motioned them to be quiet.

"It's just through those trees," he said, pointing.

Treading carefully the three moved silently towards the cabin. There was no sign of life.

Joe ducked down and moved to a spot underneath a window. The others followed. Raising their heads, they peered inside.

In the dusky room they could see nothing at first, then suddenly each receiv d a shock.

Ted Whitestone was trussed up and propped against the wall!

·16·

A Moonlight Search

SMIRKIS was standing in front of Ted, a whip held menacingly in one hand.

"You'd better tell me!" he snarled. "If you don't, you'll get more of this whip!"

"You can't get me to talk by torture!" Ted answered defiantly.

The onlookers could see several ugly welts on the boy's arms.

"Where's that buried treasure?" Smirkis demanded, using the whip on the boy's hands. "You know all right, but you and your father are trying to keep it for yourselves!"

Mike signalled the Hardys. "Okay," he whispered. "Time to move! Circle the cabin!"

Frank and Joe took up strategic positions so that Smirkis could not escape. Then, with a tremendous crash, Mike assailed the door and burst into the room!

The police officer dived for Smirkis. Though taken off guard, the wily swindler was not to be caught so easily. He slashed at his opponent with the whip, then leaped through a window.

But he was trapped. Frank and Joe converged on him from either side.

"Okay. I give up, but I can explain everything," the man declared as they led him into the cabin.

Meanwhile, Mike was releasing Ted from his bonds. The Hardys turned their prisoner over to the police officer and rushed up to Ted.

"It's sure good to see you fellows," the Indian boy said, chafing his wrists where the ropes had been fastened.

"Are you all right?" Frank asked.

"I guess you just got here in time," Ted replied soberly. Then they all turned their attention to Smirkis.

"You'd better come clean," Mike told him. "Who's paying you and what do they want?"

Smirkis hung his head. "A stranger hired me."

"What was his name?"

"He didn't tell me. He just said, 'Call me Al. I'll pay you well.'"

"For what?"

"To spy on the Ramapans. He said they had a fabulous buried treasure."

"A spy, eh?" Frank broke in. "Find out anything?"

"No," Smirkis muttered.

The Hardys wondered if he were speaking the truth.

"Where is this Al now?" Joe asked.

The prisoner shrugged.

"Where did he stay when he was in town?" Mike prodded him.

Smirkis looked at his captors sheepishly. "I let him stay in this cabin. I knew the owner wouldn't come here. Al told me he couldn't be seen in town."

"Wanted, eh?" the officer remarked.

"What did Al look like?" Frank asked.

"He's a dark, heavy-set man. About thirty-five, I'd say. He has a bad scar on the back of his right hand. Looks like a W."

"Breck!" Joe exclaimed. "Boy, does that explain a lot!"

"Good work!" the police officer said admiringly to the Hardys. "This Al or Breck—whatever his name is— we'll set a watch on this cabin, and if he shows up, we'll bring him in."

Mike took the prisoner back to town, and the boys set out for the Ramapan village.

"Did that guy talk to you all the time?" Frank asked Ted.

"No. He slept a lot, and once he went off for several hours."

"To cut the telephone line at your house," Joe deduced.

"At first he wasn't bad to me and gave me food regularly. But this morning he started whipping me 'cause I wouldn't talk."

Chief Whitestone was relieved to see his son, and Chet bubbled over with joy at seeing all three safe.

"This mystery gets more complicated," the chief remarked. "Since you've been gone, I've received a letter from that man you asked me about—Philip York."

"Philip York?" the Hardys chorused.

"He claims to be the grandson, by a former marriage of the Amos York who once owned this land. You recall we bought it from his estate."

"What did he want?" Frank asked.

"He says his father didn't get his share of the money when the property was sold."

"Has he any real claim?" Chet put in.

"If he has, we're in trouble," Chief Whitestone replied, "because all heirs have to be accounted for when any land is sold."

"Didn't the lawyers know about him?" Joe wanted to know.

"Philip York claims his father knew nothing about the deal. If that's true, then the sale of the property was illegal and the transaction has to be made all over again."

"Whew!" Joe whistled. "And you'd have to pay anything extra they might ask?"

"Yes," the chief said, frowning. "York claims he has half brothers and sisters to be paid in addition. They could insist we give them a small fortune to sign off, and we just haven't got the money."

There was silence for a few moments, then Chief Whitestone continued. "The second thing I'm worried about is a little closer to home."

"What is it?" Frank asked anxiously.

"Someone has been digging round the spot where we were looking for the buried treasure!"

"When did you discover it?" Joe questioned.

"I found bootmarks and freshly turned earth this morning, which means someone must have been there last night."

The boys gasped. "I wonder if the digger found anything!" Ted exclaimed.

Chief Whitestone tapped his pipe on the table, then

replied, "It's hard to tell, Ted. Whoever it was dug quite deep, though."

"Father, we must find out whether he was successful!"

"But how?" Chief Whitestone asked.

Almost immediately Frank came up with a plan. "We'll fool him and use a decoy."

"What kind?" Ted asked.

"The best decoy in the world," he told them. "The whole Ramapan tribe! They can put on their hunter's moon ceremonial dance this evening instead of waiting."

"I see," said Joe. "If the digger didn't find the treasure, he'll be back."

"Exactly. While everyone is watching the dance, he'll count on being alone. But you and I, Joe, will keep watch by the teepee."

"Great idea, Frank," Chief Whitestone responded, slapping the youth on the back. "I'll get the preparations for the ceremonial dance started right away."

"Say," Chet remarked eagerly, "that's really a corker of a plan after all, Frank!"

The Hardys became restless as they waited, but finally darkness fell and the brilliant hunter's moon rose like a flaming ball. Under its bright, glowing light the weird ceremony started.

First came the beat of the drums, beginning slowly, but growing more insistent. Then the dancers, dressed in war paint and feathers, started their elaborate rhythmical movements. They chanted, leaped, and twisted, as they circled the soaring flames of the great bonfire.

The dance soon got into full swing, with Indian faces

reflecting the blaze of the fire and the drums pounding wildly. Although the boys found the strange ritual fascinating, Frank finally whispered to his brother:

"We'd better go. We have work to do."

Walking stealthily they went straight to the place of the crisscross shadow. No one was about. They slipped inside the teepee and waited.

Presently Joe peeked out of the opening. For a moment all he could see was the frozen ground and the dark forest trees, still in the silver moonlight. Then he gave a sudden start.

"Someone's coming!" he reported excitedly. "Let's grab him!"

As the man came nearer, the boys rushed outside. At that moment something whizzed over their heads. A second later a large knife struck the side of the teepee.

Frank seized Joe by the shoulders and jerked him to the ground.

"That guy is trying to kill us!"

Terrified, the boys waited, their faces pressed into the cold earth. Then they heard the sound of running footsteps.

Joe stood up. "I guess the knife thrower's gone. Whew! That was a close shave! Well, at least we know the gang hasn't found the treasure yet!"

They walked back to the ceremonial dance, but found that the rite had been completed and the members of the tribe were returning home. The chief was talking soberly with a group of elderly men. Joe caught his eye and he came over in a few minutes.

Briefly, the boys recounted the experience with the knife thrower.

"I'll keep guards posted here day and night," the chief said gravely.

He beckoned to a couple of sturdy young men. After a few short commands from their leader, they stationed themselves near the teepee.

"I can use a good night's sleep," said Chet, coming up to them. He yawned.

The Hardys grinned. "All worn out from dancing," Joe teased. "You should have been dodging daggers as we were."

"Wh-wh-what!" Hearing the story, Chet said, "Wow! We'd better cut out this night work."

"We will," Frank agreed. "I'm going to phone Sam Radley to find out if he's heard anything from Dad and then hit the hay."

He picked up the phone, which had been repaired earlier.

"Mr Sam Radley, please," he said to the hospital operator. "What! He's disappeared! With a broken leg!"

Frank hung up and turned round. "Sam vanished from the hospital very mysteriously this morning. Left a cheque on the bed for his bill. No one saw him leave."

The boys looked at one another in amazement. Then Joe said, "Try his hotel. Maybe he's there."

But Sam was not at the hotel and the clerk had not heard from him.

"Maybe he's gone after the saboteurs," Chet suggested.

"More likely the gang has taken him captive." Joe said worriedly.

The three sat lost in thought for several minutes,

then Frank said, "I know somebody who might throw some light on his whereabouts."

"Who?"

"Jack Wayne. Maybe Jack took Sam on a secret plane flight!"

"You're right. Let's phone him."

Jack Wayne was a close friend of the Hardys. He owned a plane, and often piloted the boys, their father, or Sam on errands when speed and secrecy were needed to crack a case.

In a short time Frank was talking to Jack.

"W-e-l-l," Jack began, as if reluctant to reply. "I have seen Sam. Flew him on a secret mission to Chicago this afternoon."

"Did he give any details?" Frank wanted to know.

"He didn't volunteer much information, and he swore me to secrecy. All I can tell you is this: continue your investigations at the Ramapan village, and don't worry about a thing!"

Frank repeated the conversation to his brother and Chet.

"Continue our work, eh?" Joe said.

"But where?" Chet asked. "We've dug at the site of the crisscross shadow for the buried treasure, and all we have to show for it is a big pile of earth!"

"We've sure gone deep enough," Joe declared. "You know what I think? That we haven't been digging at the right shadow!"

"You've hit the nail on the head." Frank thumped the arm of his chair. "There's only one thing to do. Find the real crisscross shadow. We must do it tonight. If we wait until tomorrow, it may be cloudy.

With the moon blotted out, we'll really be stuck."

"Count me in!" Chet exclaimed. "I can always catch up on lost sleep later."

Ted and Chief Whitestone helped the Hardys in their preparations. Ted wanted to go on the search, but his father forbade this because of his exhausted condition.

Finally, equipped with hooks, picks, shovels, rope, and flashlights, the boys started off for the clearing where the teepee stood. When they arrived, Frank surveyed the area in the moonlight.

"The crisscross shadow has to be round here somewhere," he stated firmly. "If it wasn't made by teepee poles, then there must be another object which casts a shadow of the same type."

Joe pointed to the sheer side of the mountain that rose out of the clearing.

"Let's climb up there and have a look," he suggested. "We'll be able to see over a wider expanse from that height, and we may catch something we haven't noticed before."

Picking their way carefully up the steep slope, they finally reached the top of the mountain. The boys paused to catch their breath as they surveyed the whole panorama.

Their eyes swept back and forth across the scenic view below them. Intently they took in every detail, seeking the sign of the buried treasure.

"Nothing here," Frank said. "Let's look on the other side."

They walked across the level summit which was barely a hundred feet wide. The far side dropped off in a sheer cliff. Across a narrow ravine rose another steep rocky slope.

Suddenly Joe clutched the other boys' arms.

"Look!" he cried, his voice rising in excitement. "Down by that crevice in that cliff over there!"

·17·

A Parted Rope

"THE crisscross shadow!" Frank shouted.

"We've found it at last!"

"Hurrah!"

The three boys stared at a perfect crossed shadow just above a cleft in the rock wall of the mountainside facing them. It was made by two overhanging slender pinnacles of rock.

"Wait a minute," Frank said. "We've found the shadow, but it would be suicide to try climbing down to it."

"One misstep and we'd be goners." Chet shivered.

"We've got to get down there somehow!" Joe said with determination. "The future of the Ramapan tribe depends on the deed to their property! There's a narrow ledge just below us. If we could only—"

"Let's try a rope," Frank suggested, uncoiling one he was carrying over his shoulder.

He flung the end far out over the edge of the cliff. It wriggled down the stone face. The tossed coil apparently swung to the floor of the ledge, although from where they were standing the end of it was not visible.

"Quick! Tie the rope round a tree," Frank called out. "I'll go down first."

"Say, whose idea was this treasure hunt?" Chet objected. But as he gave a look downwards, he added, "On the other hand, I'd hate to be selfish."

The Hardys grinned as Joe securely tied one end of the rope to a large tree trunk. Frank tested it to be sure it would hold; then, clutching it firmly, he let himself over the edge of the cliff and, hand over hand, started his descent.

Reaching the place where he thought the ledge continued under a sharply jutting overhang, he was doomed to disappointment. Instead of a flat surface, there was a pinnacle upon which it would be impossible to land.

"It's no use," he called up.

The climb back was more difficult. The rope creaked and Joe and Chet feared it might fray apart from the constant rubbing against the rocks and toss Frank into space. But he finally made it and was hauled up the last few feet.

"Chet," Frank said, "how about your going back and telling Chief Whitestone what we've found out? He'll certainly want to throw a guard round this place until proper equipment can be brought to get down there. Meanwhile, Joe and I'll keep watch."

Chet immediately crossed to the wooded side of the mountain and began to climb down. Hindered by his bulky figure and heavy clothes, he slipped and slid, making a great deal of noise.

Rising, Chet started the trek through the woods. Suddenly he halted. He had heard a sound in the brush. The palms of his hands turned clammy as he listened intently. But he did not hear the rustling again.

Shrugging his shoulders, though his heart was hammering, Chet walked on, trying to tread as noiselessly as possible. In a moment he heard the sound once more. This time it was directly behind him!

As he swung round he was grasped roughly and thrown to the ground. A hand was clapped over his mouth. He struggled violently, but in vain.

His masked captors bound and gagged him, then carried him to a large tree.

"Okay," one of the attackers said gruffly. "You know what to do with this pest!"

"Yeah, but he weighs a ton," another protested as Chet was hoisted up to the first limb.

In a few minutes he was tied to the upper part of the tree trunk, out of sight of the ground.

"Next we'll take care of those meddling Hardy boys!" the leader declared.

When Chet heard the ominous words, he was terror-stricken. As the men moved off, he struggled to free himself, but he could not budge an inch. His heart sank as he realized that he was powerless to warn his friends.

In the meantime, Frank and Joe found a spot some fifty feet farther along the mountain where they thought they could get down to the ledge.

"Let's try it!" Joe urged. "Maybe we can hop across from there to the side where the shadow is."

They tied the rope round a tree.

"My turn this time," Joe declared.

He went down carefully, landed on the narrow

ledge, and calculated the distance to the other side.

"Okay, I'll start down," Frank called.

When he was within eight feet of the ledge, he felt the rope quiver. He looked up. His blood froze.

High above him, silhouetted against the moonlit sky, a masked face peered down at him. Alongside it was a hand holding a knife.

"Frank!" Joe cried in horror. "Somebody's going to cut you off!"

Frank reached out desperately to save himself, but it was too late. With a single swipe of the knife, the strands were severed.

Frank went tumbling through the air!

With superhuman effort Joe braced himself and caught Frank as he came hurtling down the cliffside.

But for several moments it was touch and go between life and death as they swayed and teetered near the rim of the ledge. Then Frank was able to regain his own balance.

Near exhaustion, Frank and Joe sat down, oblivious even of the taunts being called down by the man at the top of the cliff. But finally his raucous voice broke in on their thoughts.

"Now what are you going to do?" he snarled.

Another joined him and jeered at the boys, "You can't go down. You can't go up. You're trapped!"

"That's Breck!" Frank whispered excitedly.

"And York!" Joe added.

"Well, that definitely ties Dad's and our cases together!"

"Guess we'll just have to sit it out until help comes," Joe said. "Chet ought to be back soon."

But as the minutes passed and none of their friends arrived, the Hardys began to grow uneasy.

"Maybe Chet was captured," Joe remarked apprehensively.

The thought sobered them still more. Waiting made them nervous and fidgety. Finally Frank stood up.

"As long as we're here, let's cross over to the other ledge and look for the hidden papers and the dagger," he suggested.

By inching along the narrow strip they came to a place where the leap across was not too hazardous. In a few moments they were on the other side and hurrying to the spot where they had seen the crisscross shadow.

Frank chuckled. "Those men on the top of the cliff may think we've escaped."

"Let 'em think so! We'll be well screened!"

Reaching the place where the two rock pinnacles were casting their shadow in the moonlight against the cliffside, the boys could now see a narrow opening just below it.

"The papers are probably hidden in here somewhere," Frank remarked.

They took out their flashlights. Shielding the beams from any prying eyes above them, they began to search.

The two young detectives went over every inch of the rocky surface. For several minutes there was only the sound of their boots scraping the floor of the narrow opening. Then suddenly Joe gave a low cry!

·18·

A Perilous Ruse

FRANK pulled a small rusty chest from a miniature cave hidden among the rocks. He turned his flashlight on it.

After trying unsuccessfully to open the lock, Joe finally prised off the lid. From inside gleamed a million beams of light.

"The jewelled dagger!" he cried excitedly, picking up the fabulous weapon. The handle was studded with rubies, diamonds, and emeralds.

"A regular pirate's treasure!" Frank exclaimed.

"The papers are here too," Joe said, digging down for a yellowed bundle.

"See if the deed is there," Frank told him.

Joe opened a legal-looking document. He scanned it rapidly.

"This is it, Frank. The deed to the Ramapans' land!"

Just then they heard voices.

"We'd better hide this again," Frank advised.

Joe reached up and replaced the chest. Then quickly the boys scrambled out to the ledge. As they hurried along towards where they had leaped, the voices grew louder.

"Frank! Look over there! They're coming down!"

Breck and York were dangling on a long rope almost across from where the boys were standing.

The Hardys' first thought was to jump across and try to overpower their enemies, but they realized that a fight on the ledge would mean destruction for all of them. Frank and Joe decided to wait and see what the men's intentions were.

The pair had removed their masks and were cautiously making their way down the face of the cliff. The boys waited tensely.

"Maybe they're going to bargain with us," Joe said hopefully.

Frank did not agree, but replied, "We've got to outwit them. Let's try stalling them off until help comes."

"How?"

"I'm thinking," his brother answered. "We might—"

He had no chance to finish his sentence, for at that moment Breck dropped on to the ledge, and his companion followed a moment later. They jumped the span and faced the Hardys menacingly.

"Keep your distance, Breck!" Frank warned.

The boys had their shoulders to the wall of the ledge, alert for any move their enemies might make.

"Don't worry. We're not going to touch you. We'll let starvation take care of that."

"What we want to know," the other man spoke up, "is where the treasure's buried." He guffawed. "You found the crisscross shadow for us."

"What treasure?" Frank asked in a surprised tone of voice.

"Don't give us that innocent stuff," Breck growled. "You know where it is and you're going to tell us!"

"How about a little exchange of information!" Frank countered. "You give us some, we'll give you some in return."

Joe clutched his brother's arm. "You're not going to tell them, are you?" he whispered anxiously.

Frank pressed Joe's fingers in a negative signal.

"A deal, eh?" Breck sneered. "You want to make a deal when you're cornered? What's the game?" He turned to his companion. "What do you think?"

"Sure," the other replied. "What have we got to lose?"

"Okay. Shoot," Breck said to the boys.

"Tell us, then," Frank asked, "what are you really after?"

"Very simple," Breck replied. "I'm only helping Mr York here regain his rightful inheritance."

"What inheritance do you mean?" Joe spoke up.

"This land belongs to him."

"And what's more, we don't intend to let Chief Whitestone produce any papers to disprove it," York chimed in.

"We were getting along fine until you young meddlers came into the picture," Breck went on. "You almost ruined things for us, but now we've got you and your fat friend too."

"Chet Morton's been captured?" Frank cried.

"Yeah."

Joe moved forward. He wanted to choke this ruthless scoundrel. But Frank held him back.

"We warned you to lay off," Breck sneered. "But you didn't pay any attention. Thought you were smart detectives, but look where it got you."

The boys remained silent, seething as Breck recounted the story of the plot to deprive the Ramapans of their land.

"Now, you've come to the end of the line," Breck said, his voice becoming cold as steel. "You and your father."

"Where's Dad?" Frank cried.

"That you won't find out. And now how about your end of the bargain? Where's the treasure hidden?"

When the boys did not answer at once, he cried, "Come on! It's almost daybreak and we've got to clear out of here before it gets light!"

Joe looked at Frank, who was clenching his fists.

"You want the treasure, eh?" the older boy parried.

"Hurry up!"

"Walk along this ledge. You'll find a slab of rock sticking out. Turn in there and keep going. Feel round for more sharp-pointed rocks and start counting. When you get to the twelfth one, reach up."

Joe could hardly keep his face straight. How plausible Frank's story sounded!

The two men in their eagerness forgot to be cautious. While they followed directions, arguing all the way, the boys waited till they were out of earshot before speaking.

In a moment they were far enough away. Frank whispered to Joe, "The rope! Let's use it now!"

Swiftly and silently the boys jumped to the other ledge. They grasped the rope, and reeling it as they climbed, worked their way to the top of the cliff.

Suddenly there came a shout of anger from below. "Hey, you double-crossers, come back!"

As the boys scrambled to the top, Breck and York yelled curses from below.

"We've made it!" Joe exclaimed, throwing his leg over the top of the cliff and dragging himself up. Frank quickly followed.

"You have, eh?" a voice cried out.

They looked up. Three strange men, obviously armed, had them ambushed!

"If you value your lives, don't run!" one yelled.

The unequal struggle lasted only a minute. The boys were once more prisoners. Getting a close look at one of the trio, Joe whispered to Frank:

"Look at the one in the Indian suit! He's the man I shadowed that day I was attacked by Smirkis!"

"Shut up!" the man ordered.

A second one said, "You guys have given us a lot of trouble. We ought to drop you over the cliff."

Meanwhile, the rope which was tied around a tree had been let down. At that moment Breck and York appeared at the rim. It was daybreak now and in the light the boys could see their angry faces plainly.

"You lied about the treasure!" Breck yelled. "We don't go for things like that! Come on, York! We'll show them!"

He grasped Frank by the shoulder while York grabbed Joe. With the others helping, the boys were slowly but surely pushed towards the edge of the cliff!

·19·

Mousetrapped

WHEN Frank and Joe were only twenty feet from the edge, struggling with all their might against the men who were shoving them backwards towards certain death, Frank suddenly shouted:

"Time out!"

He had caught sight of two figures racing towards them. Chet and Ted!

Chet had escaped from his enemies, they thought thankfully. But now in his desire to rescue the Hardys, he was running straight into danger.

At Frank's outcry Chet stopped short and grabbed Ted. He was not exactly sure what Frank had meant by his signal call, but he interpreted it to mean that he should wait. Anxiously he and Ted slipped behind a boulder to await further instructions.

The assailants, surprised at Frank's strange words, halted also.

"What's the idea?" Breck demanded.

Frank looked him squarely in the eye. "If you still want that treasure, for Pete's sake don't push us over the cliff. You don't know where it is and we do."

"That's right, boss," one of the men said.

"They double-crossed us once. They'll do it again," Breck replied.

"We didn't double-cross you before," Frank said. "We just didn't tell you to go far enough. Listen. You have nothing to lose. We're still your prisoners."

Breck thought this over a moment. "What are you driving at?" he asked finally.

"We want to live," Frank answered.

"I say give them a chance," York spoke up. "We want those papers."

"Okay." Turning to his henchmen, Breck said, "You stay here with them. If they give you any trouble, you know what to do! York and I will go down the cliff again." He glared at the boys. "You'd better be telling us the truth this time! Where's the treasure?"

Frank had a desperate plan in mind.

"Continue from where you were before. A few yards to your left you'll see a narrow opening in the rocks. Walk five feet in there, reach up above your head, and you'll find a box."

The eyes of Breck and York gleamed with excitement. Quickly they began to descend the rope to the ledge below. The three men who stayed behind took positions in a triangular formation to guard the Hardys.

All this time Joe had been listening dumbfounded to Frank. Like the other two boys, however, he had realized that Frank had some plan. Watching closely and waiting with every muscle tense for a signal, Joe was rewarded a moment later.

"34—86X!" Frank yelled.

The secret play! Chet's number was 34. The centre poised for action!

"Hey, what's the—?" the guard on Frank's left started to say.

He got no further. The four boys rushed at their enemies. Frank, veering to the left, tackled one guard, throwing him to the ground. Joe mowed down the man on his right in a flying leap.

Chet, running pell-mell, neatly cut off the third guard who had started to the aid of the fellow Frank had attacked.

Again the secret defensive play had worked!

With the assistance of Ted's strong arms and lightning-like movements, they soon brought the fight to a close and disarmed the criminals. The captors were now the captives!

As soon as he dared leave, Frank hurried to the edge of the cliff and quickly pulled up the rope, to keep Breck and York below. Coming back to the others, he said tersely:

"Give me a hand tying these fellows up."

"We ought to take them to your father, Ted," Joe suggested.

"That won't be necessary. I'll summon help," the Indian youth answered.

Cupping his hands to his mouth, he gave a weird cry. "*Ee-ooo-ay! Ee-ooo-ay! Ee-ooo-ay!* That's the Ramapans' war cry," he explained. "Listen!"

From the valley below came an answer. "*Ee-oo-ay! Ee-ooo-ay! Ee-ooo-ay!*"

"Help will be here in a few minutes," Ted told them.

The captives, fearful of what the Indians might mete out in the form of punishment, fought like wildcats in a desperate battle to gain their freedom. But although they loosened their bonds, the boys quickly subdued them and wound the rope tighter about them.

"Well, Chet," Joe said as they dropped to the ground to rest, "tell us who captured you and how you got away."

Chet pointed to the roped-up men, then told the story of his capture.

"Ted rescued me from the tree," he concluded. "I managed to get the gag out of my mouth and then started hollering."

Ted grinned. "You certainly can yell, fellow!"

A few minutes later a band of eight Ramapans burst into view, ready for battle. They looked disappointed upon learning that their enemies already were prisoners. Ted asked six of the Indians to take the men to their village to await the police.

"You two stay here," he directed the others. "There are more of the gang below." He pointed over the cliff wall.

When the rope was removed from the prisoners, who were marched off, Frank lowered it over the rim.

"I forgot to tell you, Ted," he said, "that Breck and York will be bringing the dagger and the deed up with them."

"What!"

Frank explained the desperate chance he had taken, but there was only praise from the Indians for his action.

Joe, meanwhile, had been inching forward on his stomach until he came to the edge of the precipice. He peered over.

"They're coming!" he reported in a hoarse whisper. "Breck has the box tied to his belt!"

The impatient boys got set to grab York, who was in the lead. As his head appeared over the rim, they grasped him under the arms and yanked him up.

"Okay," he said cheerfully before he realized who his assistants were. Then, seeing them, he yelled, "Breck, they're loose!"

Breck's head jerked upward. Catching sight of the boys, he instantly started climbing down the rope.

"Stop!" Ted cried.

"You'll never get me!" screamed Breck from ten feet below them.

Frank and Joe grabbed the rope and began pulling it up. The movement caused Breck to sway out into space. He glanced downwards, and a sick look crossed his face. Then his courage returned.

"Cut it out!" he shouted. "You've got me but you'll never use these papers!"

Holding on with one hand, he began unfastening the box from his belt.

"You can't do that!" Ted cried.

"Oh no!" Breck sneered. "Watch me!"

At that instant the Hardys gave a powerful yank on the rope. With Chet guarding York to avoid a slip-up, the three Indians, holding hands, made a human chain. With one man grasping the tree, they strained forward. Ted leaned out over the cliff and snatched the box from Breck just as he was about to drop it.

"You fiends!" he screamed.

A moment later he reached the top of the cliff, too wrathful to speak further. He looked round wildly for his confederates. Not seeing them, he turned to York. But York remained silent.

"Thanks for getting the treasure for us," Chet said, relieving the tension.

The men looked on sullenly as Ted opened the box. Nothing had been disturbed, and everyone gasped upon seeing the jewelled dagger.

"And the deed—it's here!" Ted exclaimed jubilantly. "Frank and Joe, you've saved the Ramapans' home for them!"

"We couldn't have done it without you and Chet," Frank replied.

"No, indeed," Joe agreed. "We sure were in a tight spot a few minutes ago."

"Let's get started for your home with these prisoners, Ted," Frank urged. "Joe and I still have work to do."

"You mean you haven't solved the whole mystery?" Ted asked, amazed.

"There's a friend of these men I'd like to talk to."

"Who's that?"

"Miles Kamp, the lawyer," Frank replied.

The boys' prisoners flinched. Breck broke his silence.

"He's too slick for you!" he boasted. "Kamp's one of this country's cleverest lawyers."

"For certain characters," Frank shot at him. "Get moving!"

The prisoners were marched off, surrounded by their bodyguard. When they reached Ted's house, Chief Whitestone was overwhelmed. After meeting his erstwhile enemies, and being presented with the box, he fervently shook hands with the Hardys and Chet.

"My gratitude can never be adequately expressed," he said. "The Ramapans will always remember your fine and courageous work to help them. By adoption I pronounce you Hardys members of the Ramapan tribe! I understand you, Chet, already have inherited an Indian title."

"That's right," Chet replied.

"This is a great honour," the brothers said in unison and accepted their adoption with a bow.

State troopers, who had been summoned by Chief Whitestone, arrived soon afterwards and took the five captives away. Then Joe went to the telephone and called Chief Collig in Bayport. He briefly told of the recent arrests and the officer shouted his congratulations into the phone.

"That's great work, boys."

"We want you to arrest Miles Kamp at once," Joe said.

There was a snort on the other end of the wire, followed by a long throat-clearing sound.

"Joe, I'm sorry to say Kamp gave us the slip," Collig confessed.

"What!"

"My men were covering him day and night. Then, one evening, he just disappeared from his office like a puff of smoke."

"No clues?"

"None."

Disappointed, Joe hung up and reported the conversation to Frank.

"Maybe we can find out something from Breck and York!" Frank cried.

Calling a hasty good-bye to the Whitestones, they dashed for the door.

"If you don't need me," Chet spoke up. "I think I'll

stay here a little longer. I want to find out some more about Chief Wallapatookunk."

Joe laughed. "Enjoy yourself!"

Frank and Joe raced after the troopers and their prisoners and twenty minutes later caught up with them. The group paused while the boys questioned Breck and York. At first the men refused to give any help as to where the wily lawyer might be found.

"You want Kamp to defend you, don't you?" Frank asked. "How are you going to find him? He's not at his home or his office any more."

"The skunk! Why not?" York shouted.

"Well, where can we locate him?" Joe prodded.

Without stopping to analyse the situation, York burst out, "He'd better come across! I'm not going to take this rap without a fight! Tell him to come here! Look for him at his boathouse."

"Where is it?" Frank asked.

"He never told me. He said it was his special hideout when he wanted to get away from people and work on a case. But I'm pretty sure it's somewhere in Southport."

The Hardys waited no longer. They hurried to Lantern Junction, where they learned that a plane for Bayport would stop in an hour at the nearby airport.

The boys spent most of the interim at the hotel, satisfying their appetites which had been neglected for too many hours. Then they rode to the airport and boarded the plane.

Reaching Bayport, they taxied home to pick up their car. Mrs Hardy and Aunt Gertrude greeted them in surprise. The women were thrilled to hear that Breck,

York, and their henchmen had been captured but were dismayed to hear the boys were about to go after Kamp at his boathouse.

"Why don't you let the police do it?" Aunt Gertrude said. "I'll bet that waterfront is full of all sorts of wicked people."

"We'll dodge 'em all," Joe said, grinning.

The young detectives drove off, going as fast as the speed limit allowed. Reaching the Southport waterfront, they parked and started walking. The first quarter mile contained only large piers; the second quarter, the tenement district the boys had visited before.

"I guess the private boathouses are all up farther," Frank remarked.

They plodded on. As they reached the area where private boats were kept, he and Joe began questioning all the fishermen and craft owners they met. First, they would ask them if they knew where Miles Kamp's boathouse was, then inquire if they had ever seen a short, heavy-jowled man who was very near-sighted. At last they were rewarded. One workman said that although he did not know the man's name, he had seen a person who fitted the description.

"I've noticed him going in and out of that green boathouse with the apartment over the water," he said, pointing down the shore a short distance.

"Thanks."

The boys hurried along the dirt roadway at the back of the boathouses. Coming to the green one, they paused.

"Look!" Joe whispered. "On the window sill."

Frank turned. On it lay a pair of thick-lensed glasses. "I guess this is it, all right!"

Suddenly a burly man appeared from a board-walk running along the side of the apartment.

"What do you want?" he asked in a gruff voice.

"We want to see Miles Kamp," Frank said boldly.

"A message from Breck," Joe added in a confidential whisper.

The other's eyes widened. "Okay. Didn't know you were friends of his." He stood aside to let them pass and indicated the door. "Go right in."

As Frank slowly turned the knob, he and Joe exchanged glances.

This was the big test! Would they win or lose?

· 20 ·

A Victory Feast

THE boys entered the room and found Kamp lying on a sofa. A quick glance round the grimy shack convinced them that the bombastic lawyer was alone.

"Who is it?" the man asked, rising to peer at them short-sightedly. He blinked several times, then reached for his glasses on the window sill, but Joe moved them out of his reach.

"Your game is up," Frank declared grimly. "Your gang has been taken prisoner!"

"What are you talking about?" Kamp cried.

"You'd better confess," Joe said as he bound the lawyer's wrists and ankles with ropes they had carried in their pockets. The boys were running no risks that Kamp might slip through their clutches.

"Help! Help!" he cried loudly.

The guard outside heard it and rushed in.

"What are you guys up to—?" he began. Then, catching sight of Kamp's bound wrists, he roared with anger. "You tricked me."

The Hardys leaped at him. In a moment he was their captive along with his boss.

Frank now picked up Kamp's horn-rimmed glasses and adjusted them over his ears.

"The Hardy boys!" the lawyer screamed. "How did you—? What—?" He turned pale.

"Tell us your story," Frank prodded. "What was your connection with Breck and York?"

Having recovered from the shock at seeing the Hardys, he said blandly, "I don't know what you're after," he said.

"What's your connection with York?" Joe countered.

"York?" Kamp asked. "You want to know about him? Well, why didn't you say so? I'll tell you what little I know. Take this rope off."

"Not yet. You talk."

"York came to me with a story about having been cheated out of some property rights by an illegal sale to the Ramapans. I thought he had a legitimate case, so I took it. There's nothing wrong with a lawyer taking a case, is there?"

"It depends on the client," Frank replied sceptically. "What's Breck's part in the case?"

"Breck? Why, he works for me. Kind of an errand boy. I had him on this case. That's all."

"That's all, eh? We'll see about that!" A familiar voice came from the doorway.

All eyes turned to see who the speaker was, although the boys recognized the voice instantly.

"Dad!"

"Sam Radley!"

They rushed over to greet their father and his assistant, who was using crutches.

"What a relief to see you two!" cried Joe. "Dad, you don't look beat up. We were worried about you."

"I know you were, but I couldn't tell you anything."

The famous detective smiled warmly at his sons. "I'm in pretty good health," he added, winking broadly.

"How'd you know where to find us?" Frank asked.

"We stopped off at the house, and your mother told us where you'd be, so we traced you here. And not a minute too soon, I see." He surveyed the two prisoners, who glared at him.

Joe turned to Sam. "Say, why did you leave the hospital so quickly?" he asked.

"Because," Sam answered with a meaningful look at Kamp, "I had a little visit from a so-called bone surgeon. These crooks sure thought of every angle, all right!"

"You mean," Frank said, amazed, "that someone from the gang came to see you, disguised as a physician?"

"Exactly," Sam declared. "In that way he gained entrance to the hospital, having persuaded the authorities there that my doctor had asked him to examine my leg.

"It was a clever attempt at worming information from me," the assistant detective went on. "But from his conversation, I soon knew he was no doctor. I managed to evade his questions so that he wouldn't suspect I was on to his game."

"No wonder you made such a fast exit," Frank put in.

"I had to get out of there before the gang sent someone back to try more desperate means to make me talk," Sam continued. "With the help of my own doctor I was able to get some crutches and hobble away in time."

"Kamp was lying to you boys," Mr Hardy said as

all eyes focused again on the glum-faced lawyer. "Want to tell the truth, Kamp, or shall I?"

The man looked sullen and did not reply.

"Don't believe a word of that fairy tale Kamp was telling you," Fenton Hardy began. "He's no small-city lawyer. He's the legal brains of a gang of saboteurs that has been terrorizing the country! But not any longer. They've been rounded up."

Frank and Joe grinned triumphantly. They had been right about the connection between their case and the one on which their father had been working.

"The gang wanted the Ramapans' property," the detective continued, "to carry out a great plan. It's so secluded it would have made a wonderful hiding place for big-time saboteurs.

"Kamp, you hired a man named York to help you, but his real name is Philip Varry. He's a small-time crook." Mr Hardy paused to let this sink in. Then he went on:

"You got Varry to pose as Philip York, a missing heir to the Ramapan land."

Kamp studied the floor for a moment, then he raised his eyes.

"I might as well tell you everything. We planned to have Varry force a sale of the property," he said. "Whitestone refused to sell, so we had to take stronger measures.

"When we learned that the records had been burned and the Ramapans' deed was missing, I sent Varry up there to try to find it. Then you Hardy boys got involved in the case."

"Did you send us the threatening note?" Frank asked.

"Yes."

"And your men pushed us on to the railroad track?"

"That was our work. I had a friend of mine yell from the street to distract everyone's attention."

"How did you know where we were going?" Frank asked the lawyer.

"I had someone shadowing you," Kamp replied. "The morning you found the school closed he heard you talking about it. But we couldn't win.

"While Phil was in the Lantern Junction station, he stole a suitcase full of leather articles. He gave them to me, and when Breck came to make his report, I turned them over to him to use as a ruse to get into your house."

"So he *did* steal the key and hand it over to you," Joe said. "Where'd he hide it—in his mouth?"

"Yes, he gave it to me at police headquarters."

"Why did you want to get into our house?" Frank asked.

"There were letters and other documents in your father's filing cabinet that the saboteurs wanted. We could have broken in, of course, but that would have set the police on us at once."

Frank told his father about the trick that had been played on them, and how puzzled they were by the voice.

"I can explain that," Mr Hardy said. "I was on the West Coast making an anticrime movie. Part of the recording was stolen."

"Did the record say something about 'You can't beat these men. Give up!' " Joe asked excitedly.

His father smiled. "Yes it did. The whole record went like this: 'The American law enforcement agencies are the best in the world. You can't beat these men. Give up. Go home to your local communities and forget the idea that crime pays!'

"I didn't know who had stolen the recording, but you've solved that mystery too, boys. They played a vital part of the record to make you believe I was a captive. Thank goodness they didn't succeed in scaring you off the case!"

"The masquerade had us fooled for a while. We thought you were in two places at once," Frank said.

"Well, when I heard about the photograph that had been stolen from our house, it was clear that someone made up to look like me was entering factories in order to sabotage them, so I went after him.

"I didn't want to be traced, so I swore the hotel clerk to secrecy, and also the detective you put on my trail, I couldn't afford to let anyone know my plans," Fenton Hardy explained. "We can discuss the case at home, boys. Right now we'd better turn our prisoners over to the police."

At dinner Mrs Hardy and Aunt Gertrude listened eagerly to the outcome of the mystery.

"I told you right from the start Breck was a criminal!" Aunt Gertrude said smugly. "I've been working on that myself all this time."

She went for her handbag and produced a clipping several years old.

"The newspaper found this for me," she said. "Breck's never been any good. Once he was sent to jail as a confidence man."

"Nice evidence," Joe said admiringly.

Miss Hardy was pleased by the compliment and was

about to reply when the telephone rang. Frank answered. He listened a few moments. Then, after hanging up, he turned to the others:

"It was Chet. Joe, you and I are to go up to Lantern Junction to morrow to testify against Breck and Varry."

Joe grinned. "Never a dull moment."

The boys phoned Jack Wayne and made arrangements for him to fly them. Upon arriving at Lantern Junction the next morning they went straight to court, where Chet met them. The hearing was in progress. Later the Hardys gave testimony which the prosecutor said would send the swindlers to prison for long terms. And their trial for sabotage was yet to come!

After the hearing, Ted invited the boys and Jack Wayne to a farewell dinner with the Ramapans. "A real Indian feast," he promised. At the Whitestone house, he made an announcement.

"We understand Chet's great-grandfather, Ezekiel Morton, was an Indian agent here and was made honorary chief of the Pashunks who used to live nearby. We Ramapans want to honour young Chief Walla-patookunk, which we believe means *Eat-a-Whole-Moose*."

Everyone smiled.

"And now, Chet," Ted continued, "we hope you won't have any trouble imitating your great-grand-father."

A whole side of venison was carried in and set before Chet! Everyone in the room roared with laughter.

Frank and Joe were surrounded with gifts the Indians had presented in gratitude for their work in locating the deed and the jewelled dagger. The Hardys had never received a greater ovation for solving a mystery.

"Well, I guess it's back to the old dull school and football for us now." Chet sighed as he finished a third helping of venison.

"Dull? Football? Remember our defensive play 86X," Joe reminded him.

"That play pulled us through a dangerous adventure," Frank said. "Without it, the Ramapans might not be feasting us so happily tonight."

says...

'Yo-ho-ho for your next book from the Armada ship! There's a cargo of exciting reading for you—so set sail with another Armada book now.

You'll find more titles listed over the page.'

From Alfred Hitchcock,

Master of Mystery and Suspense—

A thrilling series of detection and adventure. Meet The Three Investigators – Jupiter Jones, Peter Crenshaw and Bob Andrews. Their motto, "We Investigate Anything", leads the boys into some extraordinary situations – even Jupiter's formidable brain-power is sometimes stumped by the bizarre crimes and weird villains they encounter. But with the occasional piece of advice from The Master himself, The Three Investigators solve a whole lot of sensational mysteries.

The Secret of Terror Castle
The Mystery of the Stuttering Parrot
The Mystery of the Whispering Mummy
The Mystery of the Green Ghost
The Mystery of the Vanishing Treasure
The Secret of Skeleton Island
The Mystery of the Fiery Eye
The Mystery of the Silver Spider
The Mystery of the Screaming Clock
The Mystery of the Moaning Cave
The Mystery of the Talking Skull
The Secret of the Crooked Cat
The Mystery of the Coughing Dragon
The Mystery of the Laughing Shadow
The Mystery of the Flaming Footprints
The Mystery of the Nervous Lion
The Mystery of the Singing Serpent
The Mystery of the Shrinking House
The Secret of Phantom Lake

Armada

Armada Science Fiction

Step into the strange world of Tomorrow with Armada's exciting science fiction series.

ARMADA SCI-FI 1
ARMADA SCI-FI 2
ARMADA SCI-FI 3

Edited by Richard Davis

Three spinechilling collections of thrilling tales of fantasy and adventure, specially written for Armada readers.

Read about . . . The monstrous Aliens at the bottom of the garden . . . A jungle planet inhabited by huge jellies . . . A robot with a human heart . . . The terrible, terrifying Trodes . . . A mad scientist and his captive space creatures . . . The deadly rainbow stones of Lapida . . . The last tyrannosaur on earth . . . and many more.
Stories to thrill you, stories to amuse you—and stories to give you those sneaking shivers of doubt . . .

Begin your sci-fi library soon!

Armada

CAPTAIN ARMADA

has a whole shipload of exciting books for you

Armadas are chosen by children all over the world. They're designed to fit your pocket, and your pocket money too. They're colourful, gay, and there are hundreds of titles to choose from Armada has something for everyone:

Mystery and adventure series to collect, with favourite characters and authors – like Alfred Hitchcock and The Three Investigators. The Hardy Boys. Young detective Nancy Drew. The intrepid Lone Piners. Biggles. The rascally William – and others.

Hair-raising spinechillers – ghost, monster and science fiction stories. Super craft books. Fascinating quiz and puzzle books. Lots of hilarious fun books. Many famous children's stories. Thrilling pony adventures. Popular school stories – and many more exciting titles which will all look wonderful on your bookshelf.

You can build up your own Armada collection – and new Armadas are published every month, so look out for the latest additions to the Captain's cargo.

If you'd like a complete, up-to-date list of Armada books, send a stamped, self-addressed envelope to:

Armada Books,
14 St James's Place,
London SW1A 1PF